Website: www.ehiike.com
Email address: takenaway.ehi@gmail.com
Facebook fan page:
https://www.facebook.com/takenaway
Twitter: @takenawayehi
Available @ Amazon on Kindle and Paperback

Hidden

The Sequel To Taken Away

Elli Rose,

[signature]

Ehi Ike

TATE PUBLISHING
AND ENTERPRISES, LLC

Published by Tate Publishing & Enterprises, LLC
127 E. Trade Center Terrace | Mustang, Oklahoma 73064 USA
1.888.361.9473 | www.tatepublishing.com

Tate Publishing is committed to excellence in the publishing industry. The company reflects the philosophy established by the founders, based on Psalm 68:11,
"The Lord gave the word and great was the company of those who published it."

Book design copyright © 2013 by Tate Publishing, LLC. All rights reserved.
Cover design by Junriel Boquecosa
Interior design by Caypeeline Casas

Published in the United States of America

ISBN: 978-1-62854-471-8
1. Fiction / Mystery & Detective / General
2. Fiction / Thrillers / Suspense
13.10.08

Chapter 1

I missed my mother more than I ever thought I would. I missed her massaging my scalp every night before braiding my hair. I missed the three course dinners she would make after endless nights of ramen noodles. I missed her anger, her joy…her love. I became overwhelmed with memories that lived within my mind. The only way the memories could be shown were through tears, but soon the tears became meaningless. There was nothing left to express after hours of reliving memories that felt too distant. I was unable to recall the tone of my mother's voice. I could no longer visualize a clear image of her. This frightened me more than anything: the ability to forget.

Ms. Jane had banned us from calling our families. That was our first instinct, of course. I remember our second day at her house. Brittany picked up the phone to call her father. She may have gotten three digits in before Ms. Jane realized what she was doing. She charged towards Brittany, snatched the phone away from her and roughly placed it back onto the hook. She later gave us a lecture on the importance of remaining hidden. We could not be seen through a window. We could not be heard in the house. All this so we could never be found.

The only thing I could compare this house to was a prison, but that was a vast understatement. We needed the world to believe that we were dead. After awhile, I thought we were. I began to confuse my dreams with reality. At first, dreams seemed to be the only thing that kept me going, until they turned into nightmares. My hope was gone. I feared awakening in terror, so the majority of my nights were sleepless. I shared a room with Liz. She tended to sleep well and remain calm, but I could never tell what was actually going on inside her head. She barely spoke, while Britt was unable to stop speaking. Brittany and Ashley stayed in the room beside mine. We shared a Jack and Jill bathroom. Though the beds were comfortable and the rooms were spacious, it wasn't my home.

After listening to Liz snore for hours, I left the room. The kitchen was always the place I would go when I couldn't sleep. It had wide glass windows that took up the entire wall. At night I could pull the curtains back and look outside. Ms. Jane had shutters and curtains covering most of her large windows. This was the only time I could look out of them. As I walked into the kitchen, I saw Jackson sitting at the table. The curtains were pulled back.

"What are you doing? It's three in the morning," I said.

"I could ask you the same thing." Jackson and I barely talked. It was probably our first time speaking to one another since we had been in this house.

"I couldn't sleep." I looked in the cabinet and got a cup. All of Ms. Jane's cups were glass. It was a regal environment. I don't think she ever expected to have fifteen children live in her house.

"Same." Though he never stated his feelings, I could tell Jackson missed his parents. He never tried to call, but when Ms. Jane gave us the lecture, he was one of the most infuriated. He never said anything, at least with words. I went to the refrigerator and got some water. Usually, when I was down here, I sat alone. A little company could be nice. "It sucks that we can't contact our parents to at least tell them that we are okay." Jackson looked so tired. He had huge bags under his eyes as if he hadn't slept in weeks. I avoided the bathroom mirrors, because I knew I looked the same.

"I know. We have been here for about a month, and nothing has happened. She doesn't let us watch the news. I have no idea what's going on anymore."

"I mean I understand that she wants to protect us, but this is our lives. I wish we could do something about it." There wasn't any harm in asking her. "How about we just talk to her? Let's all ask her what's going on," I suggested. Jackson's eyebrows rose.

"I mean, honestly, she is a little intimidating and moody. One moment she's nice, and the next, she's irritated with us. She would get mad about it," Jackson said. He was right. Ms. Jane was a little crazy at times, but mostly unpredictable. She could be cooking us pancakes one moment, but then something will hit her, and she would yell at us for eating them. I never knew what was on that lady's mind. I could only imagine the toll this situation was taking on her life. Not just the situation, but the secrets. "I think she is just really stressed out with what's going on. She knows everything, and she's keeping it away from us. I don't think she will yell at us for our concerns. Even if she does, Britt will just say something crude. Actually, maybe Britt should be the instigator now that I think about it." Jackson laughed.

"Haha yea, get Brittney to lead the conversation." I heard someone coming. I thought it was Ms. Jane, but she wouldn't come all the way to the third floor just because she heard something. She wouldn't even be able to hear us; we weren't loud. A tall figure walked in. It was Alex.

"What are y'all doing?" he asked. It was the first time Alex tried talking to me since the first few days we were here. Once we were rescued, everyone was excited. We were all always together celebrating, but we soon realized it was far from over. During that realization, people began alienating themselves from others. We all became distant.

"We couldn't sleep. What about you?" Jackson said. Alex walked to the refrigerator. He looked inside and got a bottle of water. He closed the refrigerator then looked at Jackson and me.

"Just thirsty." He left the kitchen. I hadn't talked to him in weeks, so I couldn't tell if he was still in that stage or not. He seemed to revolve himself around Henry and Kendall. Sometimes, I would see him, and he would be smiling and laughing with them, but it would only last for a second. I could feel it turn into a grimace. "Are you okay?" Jackson said while staring at me with concern.

"Yeah, why wouldn't I be?" I tried to fake a smile. His presence drained me.

"Well, when he walked in, you completely froze." I absolutely despised how easy it was for people to read my expressions. "Oh well, I was just amazed at how many people are up this late." I made up something. Jackson didn't need to know my indecisive feelings for Alex. I barely knew him. "Look, I know you like Alex," Jackson said. *Again, why am I so easily read?*

"It is pretty much the most obvious thing," he said. Wow, I guess everyone was under that impression.

"I honestly don't have time to even analyze anything like that."

"Mimi, we are stuck in a house with nothing to do. You have all the time in the world to think about it." He made a great point.

"We hardly ever talk. We used to be good friends, but now, he just surrounds himself with Henry and Kendall. After we moved in, he distanced himself from most people." It was pointless to pretend that I didn't like him when everyone knew I did.

"You're overanalyzing him, Mimi. I think it was hard on everyone when we first got here. We were all under the impression that this law would be overruled and seen as unconstitutional, but we haven't returned to our normal lives yet. It isn't over, and not being able to speak to our parents is a constant reminder of that."

Maybe I was over thinking it. We all separated ourselves from each other. I just didn't expect him to separate me and keep her. "And Kendall and Henry just talk to him more than you do. If you haven't realized Kendall likes him too." That wasn't really a shocker.

"How do you know this?"

"Because I know Kendall. I know how she is." I forgot that they were always together when we were on the trail. I wondered if he also felt abandoned. "But don't worry about it. He doesn't like her like that. I share a room with him and Henry, and when he talks about her, it is never in a romantic way or anything."

"Does he ever talk about me?" I couldn't believe I was worrying about this right now. After everything I've been through, I am still trying to figure out if Alex ever talks about me.

"Ask him yourself." He smirked. I didn't understand how he could be so calm right now. We almost died and now were fugitives—and he was discussing my feelings for Alex.

"Why are you so calm about this?" I asked.

"What do you mean?" He seemed confused.

"We have gone through hell for months, and here we are discussing my feelings for a boy. It just seems so stupid and immature."

"Is that all you think about: the situation we're in? Yes, we almost died, and we could be killed in any moment, but that shouldn't keep us from living right now."

"So you're saying we should make the best of our situation."

"I'm saying any day could be our last."

"Well, I guess that makes sense." To a degree, he was right, but I did think we needed to be more concerned. People were so focused on their social lives, and it was weird to me. It didn't feel right. It was silent for a minute.

"But you really should talk to Alex. Don't waste your time being hesitant."

"Why does it matter?"

"Because you will regret it." I knew I would.

"Okay, fine, but I am going to bed. I will talk to Britt in the morning about our plan. You tell all the boys, okay?"

"Okay, I will," he said.

"Good night." I walked downstairs back to the second floor of the house. I opened my door. To my surprise, Liz was wide-awake, and Ash and Britt were sitting on the bed.

"Where were you!" Britt said. It was officially four in the morning, and now they were awake for some reason.

"I got a drink of water in the kitchen," I answered.

"We heard you talking. Were you talking to Alex?" Ash said. I could not believe they were already interrogating me, and I hadn't even stepped into my room yet. I left my room all the time, and they never woke up.

"No, I was talking to Jackson."

They looked confused.

"Why? Y'all don't talk at all," Britt said.

I sat down on the bed, "He was just in the kitchen, and we talked. Not a big deal. Alex did come in the kitchen though. I didn't say anything."

"Why not?" Liz asked.

"We don't talk anymore. Sometimes, I honestly feel like he hates me," I said. They all looked at me and laughed.

"Mimi, Alex could never hate you. You do realize that, right? He probably hasn't talked to you in a while because you haven't talked to him either. Don't worry about him right now. Eventually, he will talk to you, or you will talk to him, and you guys will be fine." Ash smiled. I highly doubted that, but I did not feel like talking about it anymore.

"Well anyways," I said, "Jackson and I want everyone to talk to Ms. Jane and ask her what is going on."

They all stared at me like I was insane.

"Are you crazy? She isn't going to tell us," Liz said. "We aren't even allowed to watch the news. What makes you think she is going to tell us herself what is going on?"

"Guys, we have a right to know what is happening. She has imprisoned us, and it is not fair! If she knows that we have concerns, then maybe she will tell us what's going on. We just have to tell her that we want to know," I told them, hoping they would listen

"Okay fine." Britt said.

"Oh," I said, "and Britt that is another thing. We want you to tell her."

"What! Why me!" Her left eye seemed to be twitching.

"Because you are the only person that is not intimidated by her. Please do it!" I begged.

"Okay fine, I will, but I need you guys to have my back okay! " she shrugged.

"We will. Don't worry!" I had no intentions on leaving her side. It was my idea to begin with.

"Well, I am going back to sleep. See you when I wake up," Britt said. Britt and Ash walked back in their room, and Liz and I went to sleep.

Chapter 2

It was always so sunny when I woke up. All I saw was a burst of light coming through the window. The window in my room was small and facing the backyard, so Ms. Jane didn't feel the need to cover it up with large curtains. I liked the light sometimes, but I rarely ever slept nicely in this house, and the glimmer would always awaken me. I could get up and close the curtains, but that would take too much energy, and by that time, I would be ready to go on with the day.

I got out of the bed and noticed Liz wasn't there. She usually woke up after I did. Everyone must have been eating in the kitchen on the first floor. That meant that I had to be downstairs soon. I put on a solid blue T-shirt and some blue, workout shorts. I went to the bathroom, put my hair in a bun, washed my face, and brushed my teeth. Then I went downstairs.

"Good morning Mimi! Nice of you to join us," Ms. Jane said while cooking pancakes. Everyone was in the kitchen waiting for food, but more importantly, they were waiting for Britt to speak. I looked at Alex and Kendall. Of course, they were together. It irritated me to see them I was jealous. I was truly jealous of the time she spent with him. I wanted to spend time with Alex. I wanted to be as close as we were on the trails and I hated how much I filled my mind with dubious dreams. "Good morning, Ms. Jane." I spotted Liz and Britt in the long line for pancakes and walked toward them. Ms. Jane's kitchen was huge, but she barely had any chairs for everyone to sit down, so we usually just ate standing up.

"So, do I ask her about it now?" Britt asked. I began to feel my stomach cringe, but I couldn't tell if it was from hunger or anxiety. "I guess so," I said. "Wait, actually no—wait till I get my pancakes!"

If Britt had upset her while she was cooking, I was afraid Ms. Jane would go nuts and start throwing pancakes everywhere.

"Yeah, you're right, she might go crazy," Liz said and laughed. I finally got my pancakes while everyone was practically done eating. Britt stared at me like she expected some sort of signal.

"What?" I said.

"Do I ask now!" she yelled. Ms. Jane looked at Britt.

"Ask what?" Well, I guess she could ask her now.

"We want to know what's going on, Ms. Jane. You have us locked in this house for months, and we can't watch the news. You have it blocked! We can't do anything, and it's not fair." As Britt was talking, Ms. Jane was getting mad.

"Do you not appreciate what I am doing for y'all? I cook for you, I clean for you, I let you stay in my house. What else do you want?"

Oh boy. I should have known how mad Ms. Jane was going to be.

"Of course, we are thankful for what you are doing, but we want to know what's going on!" Britt yelled. Sometimes, Britt did not know how to talk to an adult. She didn't understand you had to be respectful and polite. Instead, Britt said whatever was on her mind in the exact way she thought it.

"I don't have enough time for this Brittney!" She started to leave the kitchen. She grabbed papers from above the refrigerator. "What do those papers say?" Britt asked.

"None of your business!" Ms. Jane yelled.

"What is Team Life? It says Team life." Ms. Jane just ran into the garage.

"Stay in the house! Do not leave, okay?" she said and got into her Lexus.

"We are not done, Ms. Jane." Britt yelled at her, but I could not tell if she heard her. She closed the garage and left.

"Thanks for having my back guys!" Britt's sarcasm was instigated by her anger.

"Hey, you seemed like you could handle her all by yourself." Alex said and laughed. He would be the one to laugh at her.

"I still needed you guys to back me up."

"Sorry, Britt, but that got a little out of control. Once she got mad, we kind of all froze," Ash said.

"Yeah," I said, "I just had no idea what to say." I really didn't. It happened so fast.

"But good job at not letting the children hear—they were in the playroom, a hallway away!" Ash said.

"Do not get mad at me for standing up to Ms. Jane. None of y'all could do it. Not even the boys!" Britt looked directly at Josh.

"Sorry, Britt! I didn't know what to do. Jackson told me you were going to do all the talking," Josh said.

Britt glared at Jackson.

"Woah, do not get me involved in your problems with your girl. I'm not in that at all," Jackson said. Britt just rolled her eyes and went upstairs. We all followed.

"But she had a sheet of paper that said Team Life." Britt stared at each step as if they had the answers.

"Yeah, I saw it too," Henry said.

"What do you think it means?" I asked.

"It's probably an organization or something. I really do not know," Henry said.

"It kind of sounds like Pro-Life," Alex laughed. He was so immature sometimes.

"Alex, you're right. It has to do with saving us," Kendall said smiling at him. It was so obvious she liked him. She just had to agree with every single thing he said.

"Why, thank you, Kendall." He winked, but Jackson did not think he liked her. I felt like I would throw up just from looking at them together. What did she have that I didn't?

"Anyways, it might be about us. We should try and find out some more information later." I walked to my room because I did not want to be in that room anymore. It was so obnoxious to see them together all the time.

"Mimi, are you okay?" I turned around. It was Ash, Liz, and Britt: the whole shebang.

"Yeah, why wouldn't I be?" I lied.

"Because Alex and Kendall are always together, and he never talks to you anymore," Britt said. She always had to be so blunt and straightforward with people. I did not even know what to say to that. It made me want to cry, but I wasn't going to—I was not going to cry over him again. I told myself, *If he likes her, then fine, I don't care.*

"What Britt means is that we will be here for you if you need us," Ash said. She was always the nice one. She understood how to respond to my feelings.

"But I have to go," Liz said. Where on earth did she have to go? We were all stuck in this mansion. It was not like we could leave.

"Where?" I said with a confused look.

"Well, Jason is getting mad at me. I kind of ditched him for you guys before we were rescued. He got upset because he has been pretty alone."

I vaguely remembered Jason. He talked one time at one of our meetings while we were trying to find a way to escape. That was who Liz talked to before I met her.

"Who the crap is Jason?" Britt said. I found it kind of sad that Britt had no idea who everyone was. Liz just rolled her eyes and walked out of the room. "Seriously," Britt said, "who is Jason?"

"He is Liz's friend. They would always walk with each other on the trails," Ash said.

"I do not remember a Jason. I do not think I have even seen a Jason this whole entire time."

"Just forget it, Britt. It's okay," I said. She was still confused and frustrated.

"No, I want to know who this Jason is?"

Someone knocked on the door. No one ever knocked on our door, simply because no one ever came in our room, besides us.

"It's Alex." My heart stopped. Britt opened the door.

"Hey, Alex!" she said cheerfully.

"Come on, Brittney. Let's go find Jason," Ash said. She grabbed Britt and ran out of the room before Britt even had the chance to say something.

"Hey," I said. I didn't make eye contact with him. I didn't know what to say or do.

"Hey," he said and walked in and sat on the floor across from me. "So, why were you talking to Jackson at four in the morning last night?" Of course, he wanted to ask me about Jackson. He hadn't talked to me for weeks, but once he saw me talking to someone else, he was concerned.

"Why, is it a big deal?" I said.

"Just asking, Mimi. Geez, don't get so mad," he said.

"I couldn't go to sleep, so I went into the kitchen, and he was there," I said.

"Oh."

"Yup."

"So, do you like him?" Oh goodness! Alex always had to jump to conclusions immediately.

"No! Why do you think that every single guy I talk to I like? First Chase and now Jackson!" I yelled. He was just so frustrating. He just laughed at me hysterically. "What? Why are you laughing?"

"I forgot how irritated you would get with me. I kind of missed messing with you." He kept laughing.

"Whatever." I rolled my eyes. I was probably being mean to him. I guess I was just so irritated with him hanging with Kendall all the time.

"Finally," he said and smiled, "you rolled your eyes."

"You have no idea how annoying you are." He was always being so irritating.

"Oh please. You love it."

"You wish." I laughed. Sadly, it was true though. If he didn't, I didn't know what I would do.

"Wow! I got you to smile!" he said. I didn't understand why that was a big deal, since I was usually smiling.

"I smile all the time," I said.

"You seem pretty upset right now."

"Well, I'm not." I lied, as usual. I was full of so much jealousy; I thought my head would explode.

"Okay, whatever you say, Mimi. But seriously, do you like Jackson?" *Here we go again.*

"No, Alex. We are just friends, and a boyfriend is the last thing on my mind."

"Okay. I believe you." He smiled. I missed his smile so much. I missed everything about him. I wanted to hug him, but I didn't know if that would be weird or not, but I did it anyways. "What was that for?" he asked.

"I strangely missed you," I said. All of a sudden, Kendall opened the door. She could have knocked.

"Alex! I have been looking for you!" She had the widest grin on her face.

"Well," Alex answered. "I have been right here this whole time."

She walked into my room and sat on the floor beside him.

"You promised you would watch this movie with me," She said. I wanted her to get out of my room right now.

"Oh yeah, Mimi, do you want to watch it with us?" I pretended to debate it in my mind, but the answer was obvious.

"I think she is fine in here. You like sitting in here by yourself, don't you?" Kendall said to me and smiled. At first, the only reason why I did not like this girl was because she was all over Alex. I didn't realize how fake she was: she comes into my room pretending like I don't even exist, and then, she answers for me.

"I don't really want to watch a movie right now," I said to Alex, ignoring Kendall.

"Are you sure?" he asked.

"She said she's fine, Alex," Kendall didn't even give me a chance to respond. "Let's go!" She got up and pulled him up from the floor and left. I hate her.

"Mimi," someone called me. I turned around, and it was Chase.

"Hey, Chase," I said. This was weird. Chase never talked to me.

"Do you know where Ash is?" He and Ash were still together, but I didn't think he was good for her. "I think she is somewhere with Britt, but I don't know."

"Yeah, this house is so big. I can't even find my girl-friend." He laughed.

"Yeah." I expected him to leave, but he was still standing by the door.

"Is there something you want?" I asked him. He walked into my room and sat on the floor next to me.

"How are you Mimi?" he asked. "Are you okay?" I began to feel uncomfortable.

"Yes, I am fine," I said to him. "Why?" I got off the floor and went to the bed.

"It just seems like you have been depressed," he told me. "I want you to know that we are friends, and we can talk about anything." He got up and went to the bed too.

This was really weird.

"Well, I'm good Chase," I said.

"You can tell me anything," he said. "I am here for you."

"That's great to know."

"Because I care about you, and we are friends." I was officially creeped out. This was so weird. I barely talked to him.

"Okay, Chase." I got up and walked away from him.

"We are friends, right?" He got up and followed me.

"Of course." I walked by the door.

"Okay, good." He smiled and followed me to the door.

"Well, you should probably go find Ashley," I said to him. "Bye." I closed the door on his face and locked it. Finally, I was alone in this room.

Boom. Boom. Seriously. I can never be alone. Someone has to come into the room and talk to me right now.

"What?"

I opened the door. It was Jackson.

"Sorry," he said. "I can come another time." I didn't mean to yell at him. After speaking with him last night, I trusted him. It didn't make logical sense to trust someone after one conversation, but something made me. It could have been his insight, or his honesty, but I felt comfortable around him. I felt I had found a friend. "No, sorry! I thought you were someone else. Come in." He walked while I collapsed onto my bed. I was exhausted.

"Are you tired?" he asked.

"Extremely!" I answered. "You know your friend came in here today."

"Who?"

"Kendall. I was talking to Alex, and she just comes into my room without knocking and takes him then leaves. She completely ignored me."

"Hmm...it sounds like someone is jealous."

"She is just annoying," I said.

"She's jealous of you too, ya know." That was actually shocking. She spent the most time with him.

"Why? She is always with him."

"She has to work to get his attention, and Alex always comes to you. I know you think he is always ignoring you, but if you really think about it, you never try to talk to him. The reason why Kendall is always with him is because she tries to be." He was right, she really did come off that way.

"I guess you're right."

"I know."

"He came in here and asked me if I liked you."

Jackson looked at me like I was crazy.

"Are you serious?"

"Yeah."

"It's probably because he cares about you."

I was aware of that. I just felt like it's more of a sisterly way. I j didn't want to just be a sister to him.

"He views me as his younger sister," I said.

"I am not sure how he cares about you, but if it is in a sisterly manner, at least he does care about you. You will just have to move on."

He was kind of harsh, but I appreciated his honesty. He seemed to always have the right answer.

"So what happened between you and—" Britt stopped. It was Ash and Britt back in the room. They saw Jackson and looked confused.

"He left with Kendall."

"So why is he in here?" Britt said. Ash shoved her.

"I was leaving," Jackson said.

"You don't have too!" I said. Britt was so crude sometimes.

"No, it's fine," Jackson said, and as he walked to the door, he smiled at Ash. Ash politely smiled Britt smiled, but he walked out and ignored her. I didn't blame him.

"What is wrong with you? You are always so rude," Ash said.

"I didn't do anything?" Britt shot back.

That made me think: *was she really that oblivious to her actions?*

"You were really rude to him," I said.

"Mimi," Ash said to me, "she was worst to Jason. We found Jason and Liz together, and she goes up to Jason talking about how she had no idea he even existed." Ash looked at Britt. "You don't say that to a person, Britt. You were also rude to Ms. Jane too. You can't do that. She saved us and let us into her home. You can't just be that disrespectful to her."

"I'm not even supposed to be here!" Britt yelled. We got quiet. I understood now. I forgot that her parents made more than fifty thousand a year. "I'm sorry guys, but I just miss my family. I miss my parents more than anything, and they probably feel horrible. I know it sounds awful, but you just don't understand how frustrating that is."

"I'm sorry, Britt," I told her. "I didn't know this was going to happen."

"It's not your fault, Mimi." She thought it was though. There was no way Britt didn't resent me for inviting her to my house.

"Yes, it is," I said.

She was at my house that day we got kidnapped. She was never supposed to be in this position.

"It was my decision to go to your house," Britt said. "Don't blame yourself, Mimi. If I didn't get taken away, I don't know what I would have done. My two best friends would be gone. Josh would've been gone. I don't regret the fact that I went to your house that day. Know that, Mimi, and I don't pity myself for being here. I love you guys, and I don't know if I could live without y'all. I just miss my parents. I know they are worried about me, especially since I wasn't meant to be in this position. They probably think I am dead right now, and I can't tell them I'm okay."

Tears were falling down our faces. There was nothing left to be said. It was one of those moments that I felt everything, but words limited me. Maybe it wasn't the words, but the courage to speak them. Saying sorry didn't makeup for losing her family and her rights when she wasn't supposed to. Saying she didn't resent me, didn't change my belief that she did. Our perpetual perceptions would never make an objective reality. Guilt would constantly eat at me, while Britt denied my reason for feeling it. So we would be left in silence, too afraid to say anything.

Chapter 3

I could hear the garage door opening. Ms. Jane was back. I was not certain on how Ms. Jane would act after the incident earlier. She was so unpredictable. "Oh, great! She's back. What do you think she's going to do?" Britt asked.

"I'm not sure," I answered, "but let's go downstairs and find out?" I got up. Britt and Ash followed. I heard someone humming in the kitchen. It was Ms. Jane. She was cooking something on the stove.

"Hey, girls!" Ms. Jane called us out. "Guess what we're having today—baked chicken and steamed brown rice. You will love it!" She was overwhelmingly joyous.

"I knew she would get over it," Britt whispered to Ash and I. Ms. Jane looked up from her pot.

"What was that Britt?" Her voice turned stern. "Oh, nothing, I just said it smells good!" When Britt tried to hide something, she over exaggerated her words making it obvious she was hiding something. Luckily, Ms. Jane didn't notice anything; she is oblivious to so much when it came to us.

"We're going to go back upstairs!" Britt began to run upstairs.

"Tell everyone dinner will be ready in an hour. Thank you!"

"No, Ms. Jane," Ash began. "Thank you for this fantastic meal." I knew what Ash was doing. She was trying to be nice to makeup for Britt's behavior earlier. I just smiled at Ms. Jane. She got the message.

"Hey, girls. I want you to know that everything I do is to protect you. Trust me." She grinned.

It was difficult trusting her when she kept so much from us. After the trails, it was hard for me to trust any adult. I had to remember, she saved my life. She rescued everyone. Maybe everything she did was for our benefit. Ms. Jane lived in four-story house. She had no children, no animals, and very few friends. I never understood the significance of living in a house this large without a family. I knew it wasn't about the status for her, but now this house was filled with fugitives. She had no experience with children or teenagers, let alone fifteen of them. She was doing the best she could. I watched her place a chicken breast into the pan. Her eyebrows rose as it sizzled. She placed another breast into the pan, and her lips began to curl. With each chicken breast she added, her mouth curled until it turned into a full grin. She wasn't eating alone. So I told myself, I can depend on her, but there was something missing. There was an intangible gap between us and maybe she created it for our safety. "So," Britt said, "I think she is still mad at me."

"Then you should have apologized," Ash said.

"I didn't want to bring it up! That would have been awkward."

I agreed with Britt. Ms. Jane never brought it up, so I might have been the same way.

"You're probably right," I said, "but you know she only wants to protect us. She believes it's in our best interest if we don't know."

"I don't really agree with that at all," Britt yelled. "You can't just keep people in the dark."

"Calm down, Britt. I understand not telling the children. They are so young, and they would be mortified if they knew the truth." Ash eyes began to water.

"That did not turn out so well last time," I said. "Do you not remember John and Andrew listening to our meetings? I am not saying we tell them, but if they ask, let's not lie this time."

"Agreed," Both Britt and Ash said.

The door opened. It was Liz.

"What are you guys agreeing on?"

"Liz! Where have you been?" Britt asked. Liz "I was just with you like two hours ago in the kitchen." Britt was turned off by Liz's lack of an energetic response. "So what did y'all agree on?" Liz asked.

"We talked to Ms. Jane. She told us word for word: 'everything I do is to protect you, trust me,'" I wanted to see if Liz would believe Ms. Jane or not.

"That makes sense," Liz said.

"But we want to know what is going on!" Britt continued to raise her voice.

"I said it makes sense. I didn't say I agree," Liz said.

"So what do you think we do?" Britt asked. "Should we continue to follow her?"

"Of course, we do! Just because we follow her doesn't mean we have to obey everything she says. We can find a way to get some answers."

Liz was right. There were plenty of ways we could find out what was going on, but I couldn't think of one. "Dinner is ready!" someone yelled. We all went downstairs to the kitchen. I saw the little kids in our chairs. Normally, anyone over 14 sat at the table. Someone bumped into me with a pot of chicken in their hand.

"We're eating in the other kitchen," Henry said to me. Hearing Henry's voice gave me chills. He was another person I hadn't spoken to and I missed him. He was one of the most mature kids here—except he wasn't a kid anymore.

"Oh, okay, thanks!" I saw all the guys carry food. Chase was carrying a large container of rice, Jackson was carrying broccoli, and Alex was carrying dinner rolls—and Kendall was helping him. Of course, she was. I went to the third floor. Henry was placing the chicken on the table, and Jackson was putting the broccoli on the kitchen counter. The table was so much bigger than the kitchen on the first floor. It could fit twelve people.

"Mimi," Henry said, "get the plates and set them up." This was second time he talked to me. I didn't know what had changed, but I was glad. Alex and Henry were making their way back into my life. "Alex, you should sit with me." Kendall did try exceedingly hard to get Alex's attention, but she was successful. I got the plates from the cabinet and set them on the table.

"Thanks, Mimi." Alex smiled. I could see Kendall tightening her grip on her fork and I must say, I was satisfied.

"No problem." I sat across from Alex and next to Jackson and Liz. The best advantage about living in this house was Ms. Jane's cooking. Her food was always incredible. It was awkward at the dinner table. Everyone focused on eating to break the silence with loud chewing. No one knew what to say. I could see everyone staring at someone. Jackson stared at Ash, but once she noticed, he would look away. Ash would shrug and go back to eating her food, but then again, Jackson would stare at her. This process would continue.

"Okay, it is way too quiet. Someone talk!" Britt broke the peaceful yet awkward silence. I laughed and continued slicing my chicken with my fork.

"Mimi," I saw Alex squinting at me, "what are you doing?"

"I'm eating."

"You cut your chicken and sprinkle it on top of your rice?"

"Um, yes."

He laughed.

"What's so funny?" I asked.

"That is so weird!" He kept laughing.

"No, it's not! Try it," I demanded.

"Never," he said.

"It won't kill you, Alex. Just try it."

He put his chicken on his rice. I was surprised he backed down so easily. "This is actually good," he said, "but it is still weird."

"Yeah, it is," Kendall said, "I hate my food touching." She looked at Alex smiling, but he paid her no attention. He just continued to eat. I think Alex was finally beginning to realize how annoying she was. "Anyway, how was everyone's day?" Britt asked.

"Well, we have been stuck in this house for weeks which is boring, but we're still alive, so that's a plus," Josh said.

"Cheers to that," Alex said and laughed. I heard someone coming from the stairs.

"Hello, kids!" It was Ms. Jane. She sat at one of the empty chairs, "Just wanted to make sure you guys were enjoying the food."

"The food is really good, Ms. Jane," I said. "Thank you so much!" Everyone nodded their heads and agreed. She seemed flattered.

"Thank you!" She calmed down. "I need to talk to you all about this morning. I want y'all to understand that I care about you. I want you to feel comfortable here. I know it's not your real home, and I know you miss your parents, but I want you to know I am always here for you." She was never this sentimental—happy but not sentimental. She usually just gave us our necessities, but she always kept her distance. I knew now that she just wanted to protect us but also herself. She held back for fear of losing, and the gap continued to grow. "Ms. Jane," Ash said, "we are so thankful for everything you have done for us."

"You have given us your house and a place to stay safe," Britt said to Ms. Jane. "I'm sorry for this morning. I didn't mean to disrespect you, but I think it is really important for us to know what is going on. I know you want to protect us, but I think we have the right to know." Britt just had to ask. At least she apologized.

"I understand your need to know everything that is going on right now," Ms. Jane said, "but you guys need to trust me. The less you know, the safer you are." Ms. Jane never remained this calm with Britt. "I have to agree with Britt," Josh said. "I know you believe that is true, but we are a lot stronger than you think. I mean, we were supposed to be dead months ago and were still alive," Josh said. Britt mouthed thank you to him.

"I am eighteen now," Henry said. "This law doesn't include me anymore."

That got Ms. Jane quiet.

"Since it was passed before you were eighteen," Ms. Jane said, "it still includes you."

"I can still help Team Life," Henry said. Ms. Jane looked down. "They're looking for us," he said, "aren't they?"

That made sense why she would want to keep everything away from us. She didn't want us to be afraid of being found and killed.

"No!" she shouted. "Just forget we ever had this conversation, okay?" Ms. Jane was frustrated. We were getting closer to finding out what was going on, and she couldn't lie about it.

"Ms. Jane. Please tell us," I asked. She stood up. There was sweat dripping from her forehead. Her eyes reminded me of a little girl frightened to tell her parents about a bad grade on her report card. Ms. Jane held on to her secrets. Her body remained stiff, keeping her from making any movements, but she couldn't stop her chest from raising and deflating every second. "I have to go. You guys need to go to bed." She started to turn around and head for the door.

"Ms. Jane, please." She froze again

"You guys need to go to bed," she said to us. "Good night." She left. "Is she gone?" Britt whispered.

"I think so," Liz responded.

"Okay, good! So Liz and I decided that we need to start having our meetings again. She may not feel comfortable telling us the information, but I'm certain we can find it ourselves. We need to devise a plan." Ms. Jane was close to breaking, but there was no need to push her anymore. Things were probably more hectic now than ever. We had no information, and no one to help us find it. We had to find the information ourselves and take control of this situation.

"Woah!" Kendall said. "Wait a minute, you want us to go behind Ms. Jane's back and look for all of the information ourselves?" Kendall obviously did not approve.

"Sounds good to me," Alex said.

"Oh yes, it's a great idea!" Kendall said. "Good plan!" I rolled my eyes.

"Okay, great!" Britt said. "I think we should meet in the kitchen from now on." She was so excited.

"So, are we starting now?" Josh asked Britt.

"Um…I guess. After we do the dishes, we can start. It's not my turn, so I am not doing them."

"It's not my turn either," Josh said.

"Nose goes!" Alex yelled. Everyone put their finger on their nose except me. I was too late.

"I guess I will do them," I said.

Everyone laughed.

"I'll help you," Alex offered.

"I'll help too." Kendall followed.

"I think we only need two people," Alex said. Though I had been enjoying her rejection, I knew how she felt.

"Oh, okay," she said to Alex. "Well, I'll talk to you later." Everyone got up. Alex went with me to the sink, and everyone else put their plates on the kitchen counter. Jackson walked away with Kendall. I guess he wanted to help her. He appeared to be good at that.

"Where's the detergent?" Alex asked me.

"Under the sink."

He looked under the sink and got the detergent. He filled the sink halfway up with water, while pouring a few drops of detergent into the sink.

"I wash. You dry," Alex demanded. There was no way I was letting him wash.

"I don't trust you with the water," I told him, "so I will wash, and you will dry." I reached to get the rag, but he pulled his arm back.

"You don't trust me," he said, "Now, why is that?" He grinned. "You will make a mess and get water everywhere! I know you Alex."

He laughed.

"And I should trust you?" he said. "You're the younger one."

"And you act younger."

"Oh, wow, Mimi. I didn't realize you felt this way." His annoying sense of amusement was not entertaining. "Shut up." I reached for the rag. While he pulled away, I slipped and almost fell, but he caught me.

"Are you okay?" That was the first time I heard concern in his voice. It was comforting to see a pensive side of him. For once, he wasn't acting like a child. "Mimi?"

"Yeah, I'm fine." I didn't realize he was still holding me. I got up and took the rag and started washing the dishes.

"I see you're still clumsy." He laughed. I should have known his concern was not going to last more than five seconds.

"I'm working on it."

"You need to work harder."

"You know not everyone is perfect. People have flaws. But of course, you don't Alex. I forgot no one is as amazing as you." I tried to sound sarcastic. Surprisingly, it wasn't that hard.

"I'm glad you're finally realizing this." He always had the ability to make me roll my eyes with every response he gave.

"Relax, Mimi," he said. "I'm just kidding."

I just rolled my eyes again. He didn't respond. It got quiet for a while, but I had to ask him the question that was bothering me. It would not get out of my head.

"So what is up with you and Kendall?" I asked. I tried to sound calm. "We're just friends."

"You guys have been spending a lot of time together."

"Coming from the girl who always yells at me when I see a guy talking to her and assume something is going on."

"That is different."

"How so?" He stopped drying and stared at me with the same irritating smirk he has.

"You will see me talk to Chase or Jackson one time, and freak out. You and Kendall are always together and don't deny it."

"Well," he couldn't deny it, "she kind of follows me a lot, but it doesn't bother me." I was hoping it would. "Besides, why does it matter?" He mimicked my voice from earlier when he asked about Jackson.

"I was just asking."

"Aw," he said, "I think someone is jealous." Alex was full of himself.

"Don't flatter yourself, Alex. You are not as great as you think you are."

" Lies." He laughed. "You should hang out with us."

I hope he wasn't serious. There was no way I was hanging with them to.

"Why?" I said. "I think she hates me." I was completely fine with her hatred toward me because it was equivalent to mine toward her.

"No, she doesn't. Just talk to her."

"I think I will be fine."

"You need to leave your room," he told me. "You're always in there, and I don't know why because there are tons of things you could do outside of it."

"Aw, you sound worried."

"Don't flatter yourself, Mimi," he said. "You are not as great as you think you are."

"Lies." I laughed. We were finally done with the dishes.

"Seriously though," he said, "I'm the only person Kendall feels comfortable around besides Henry and Jackson. She feels like you girls are exclusive."

I never actually thought about that.

"She never has tried to talk to us," I said. It was true though. I didn't think Kendall had any interest in Liz or Ash.

"Are you guys done?" Britt yelled.

"Yes, Brittney," Alex said.

"Good!" Everyone else came into the kitchen. "Okay, guys. We need to come up with a plan to get more information about this Team Life."

"She probably doesn't keep any information in her house," I said. "She knows we would go through it and find out."

"Or she might keep it in her office," Henry suggested. "Ms. Jane probably wouldn't want to carry around a ton of information about us to her work. We are illegal fugitives."

"Doesn't she keep it locked?" Kendall asked. She was right next to Alex again.

"We will find out," Alex said.

"What about her room?" Chase asked.

"I highly doubt she will have anything in her bedroom. It's too personal." I agreed with Alex.

"Her office is personal too," Ash said.

"But her office doesn't have clothes, shoes, and purses with money," Alex responded.

"Okay, great!" Britt said. "We will sneak into her office tomorrow after she leaves for work."

"Sounds great to me!" I said.

Everyone seemed satisfied.

"Okay, we will continue this tomorrow. Good night, everyone!" I could tell Britt enjoyed leading everything. She had this power that she honestly deserved. I walked to my room. Once I laid on my bed, I completely passed out.

Chapter 4

"Mimi, wake up!" Liz yelled at me. I opened my eyes. It was incredibly bright, and the sunlight from the window was too much to handle.

"Five more minutes."

"No, Mimi. I will give you five minutes to get ready! We planned to break into Ms. Jane's office today, and she just left. Everyone is waiting for you, but if you would rather sleep in longer, then we can start without you." I completely forgot about our plan.

"Wait a little bit longer. I have to brush my teeth!"

"Just hurry up! I told everyone I would get you up in five minutes, and it has been three." I had never heard Liz so impatient. She was starting to sound like Britt—which wasn't exactly the greatest thing in the world.

"Brushing!" I said while shoving a toothbrush in my mouth full of toothpaste, while washing my face with a washcloth. I was not the best at multitasking. "One more minute." Then I was ready.

"Done!"

"Good," she said. "Now, let's go!"

She ran downstairs, and I followed her.

Ms. Jane's office was right near the garage. Everyone was in front of the door trying to figure out how to unlock it.

"I thought you said you knew how to unlock a door without a key?" Josh was hovered over Britt, as she tried to pick the lock with a paper clip.

"This lock is different."

"Well, figure it out."

"How about you try unlocking it and see how fun it is."

Josh remained silent.

"Here," Henry said, "let me see." Britt moved out of his way so that he could look at the doorknob. "Give me the paper clip." Britt gave it to him. He started to play with the lock on the doorknob.

"Are you getting anywhere?" Britt asked. "Is it working?"

"Give me a minute."

"What's going on? Do you know what you're doing?" Britt continued to ask him questions. Henry stopped and looked up at her. I didn't think he had ever realized how annoying Britt could be when she was really anxious.

"Can you be patient?" Henry said calmly. Britt nodded. "Thank you," he said and went back to using the paper clip to break into the door. "Maybe a safety pen would work better." Britt had one in her pocket and then gave it to him. He started to use the safety pin. "Never mind, the paper clip is better." He gave her the safety pin back.

"Are you sure you know what you're doing?" Britt asked again.

"Brittney." I could tell he was getting frustrated with her, and he was going to let her know, but Britt interrupted him.

"Sorry! I won't ask anything else. I promise." I was really surprised Britt apologized. She never apologized for being herself.

"Got it," Henry said. He opened the door.

"Yes! I knew you could do it!" Britt said, even though she doubted him the entire time. She wrapped her arms around Henry's waist. It seemed like Henry didn't know what to do with his arms. He was surprised that Britt would even be hugging him after she nagged him for trying to open the door. He slowly wrapped his arms around her, and awkwardly patted his right hand on her back. "Okay," I said, "let's see what is in here." We walked in, and it was a spacious room. She had a bookshelf, a desk, and a table. It was neat and organized.

"I'll check the bookshelf," Alex said. I checked with him. Many of Ms. Jane's books were economic books. Some were college textbooks, and the others were biographies of really successful people like Bill Gates and Steve Jobs. I saw a few pieces of literature by Herman Melville, Tom Sawyer, and others by Fitzpatrick, and Hemingway—but there was no information on Team Life.

"I don't think there is anything here," I said to Alex. He turned around and looked at everyone else.

"Have you guys found anything?"

"Nope," Jackson said. He was with Kendall searching her table.

"All of it is just information on her job. Maybe she doesn't keep anything about Team Life in here."

"We have been searching for five minutes. Keep looking," Britt demanded. I could tell she felt empowered.

"Hey, guys," Josh said. "This door is locked." There were two doors off against the wall. It looked like it was the opening of a closet, but I was not sure.

"I wonder why she would want to keep it locked," Jackson said.

"Henry," Britt said, "go do your thing," she demanded again. Henry hesitated but went to the door and started to try to unlock it.

"This one is harder," he said.

"Maybe it has the information about Team Life," Ash said.

"Agreed. I don't think she would have gone through so much trouble to lock that door if it didn't," Chase said. I noticed everyone was starting to wait on Henry to unlock the door.

"Everyone, continue searching!" We all followed Britt. I kept searching the bookshelf even though there was nothing there.

"Let's check her desk," I told Alex. But Ash and Chase were checking the desk already.

"I think they got it covered."

"There is nothing to do at this bookshelf," I said, "so let's go on and help." I opened her top drawer. There was nothing but a stapler, highlighter, pen, and a few papers. Alex grabbed the papers and went through them.

"It's just printer paper." Alex shrugged.

"Don't worry," I said, "We will find something."

"Hey, what are you guys doing?" I looked up, and it was Andrew and John. "Hey, cutie." Andrew winked at me.

"Get out of here!" Liz yelled.

"No," John said. "We want to know what is going on?" I liked John. He seemed mature for his age unlike Andrew.

"I'm older, and when Ms. Jane is gone, you guys listen to me," Britt said.

"Why, you never even talk to us," John said. "We are usually in the playroom by ourselves. Ashley and Mimi are the only ones that ever checked on us. I say this with all the respect in the world, but you don't do anything for us. We do everything on our own. We know you are hiding something from us, and just because we are a few years younger, does not mean we can't know. You tried to keep things away from us last time and look how that turned out. Just tell us what's happening right now."

"Yeah!" Andrew agreed.

"Honestly," Ash said, "we don't know. Ms. Jane won't tell us anything either."

"Ash, hush!" Britt said.

"You're lying," Andrew said.

"No, we aren't!" I said. "She blocked all of the news channels. Why do you think we are in here looking through all of her things?" They got quiet. "Listen, I understand how you feel because that's how we feel about Ms. Jane. She won't tell us anything, but I promise we won't keep you out of the blue this time. If we find out anything, we will tell you, all right?"

"We can help y'all search." John offered.

"I think it is best if we look," Ash said. "You might not completely understand everything."

"Okay," Britt wait for John and Andrew to leave. They walked out and closed the door. Britt locked it behind them. "Are we really going to tell them?" Britt asked.

"I'm not sure," I said, "but they have a right to know."

"We don't have any information yet," Jackson said, "so let's just focus on that."

"Henry, are you still working on that lock?" Britt asked.

"I kind of got a little distracted by those kids," he said.

"It's okay, just keep up the good work." Britt smiled and patted him on the shoulder. Henry was confused by Britt's urge to touch him.

"What?" she said.

"Nothing," Henry said. He continued to unlock the door.

"Okay, everyone back to work. The kids are gone, so let's get some answers." I really don't know how Britt became the leader, but she was and people were actually listening to her. Alex and I continued to look through other draws. I checked the bottom draw. It was full of files.

"What is this?" Alex asked.

"Let's see." Each file had a name on it. I pulled out one. It said "Alexander Wary" in bold letters. "She has our files," I said. "How on earth does she have our files?"

"I guess she did a background check on all of us," Alex said.

I pulled out my file. It had my report cards, the schools I attended, my parents and their occupation. She knew everything about me.

"She has everything on here," Alex said.

"I know!" I exclaimed. "This is kind of weird."

"No, Mimi. She has everything about my biological parents." I could see

"Oh. Are you okay?" I asked.

"Mimi," Alex said, "my biological mother had a sister. She was supposed to have custody of me, but instead, she put me up for adoption."

I knew that Alex's foster parents weren't the best in the world. "Why didn't she want me?" Alex's eyes were watering. I had never seen him like this. I didn't know what to do. The only thing I could do was hug him.

"Maybe she did want you," I said to him. "Maybe she was too young to take care of you. I don't know but don't think she didn't want you." He pulled my arms away and placed the file onto the desk.

"I don't want to look at these anymore."

"Okay," I said, "well then, we don't have to." I knew I could never talk about his parents. It was a sensitive subject, and now finding out he had an aunt- Alex started to leave the room.

"Where are you going?" I asked. He continued to walk away. I followed.

"Wait, Alex! It's okay." I tried hugging him, but he grabbed my hands.

"No, it's not!" he said. "None of this is okay. The government wants us dead and we are fugitives living in a mansion owned by a lady who has every record of us in her office. She knows more about us than we know about ourselves. She can't be trusted."

I could see his veins popping out of his skin. "Alex, she saved our lives. She saved our lives. I understand your up—" Alex interrupted me.

"No, you don't understand! You don't understand anything. You don't know what her intentions are. She could be saving us to make herself look like a hero in the end. This could be some kind of strategy for her to make more money. We don't really know what her motive is." He was beginning to scare me.

I had never seen him so angry in my life.

"Alex, I know you're mad. Just calm do—" he interrupted me again.

"Don't tell me to calm down! You don't know me at all! You've been around me for what, a few months? You don't know me, and you have no right to tell me to calm down!"

He went upstairs. I didn't know what to do. I didn't know what to say, and even if I did, I couldn't say it. I could barely breathe. I wanted to be there for him, but he was pushing me away. I cared about him so much. I never thought he could get that angry. I walked back to the office. I could barely see the door. Everything was so blurry. I opened the door and everyone was standing there listening.

"Mimi," Britt said, "are you okay?" She ran up to me and hugged me. I tried to respond, but I couldn't. I realized tears were falling down my face.

"What happened?" Ash asked. "What is he mad about?" I still couldn't speak.

"Mimi, calm down." Liz said. I listened to her. Everyone was staring at me like I was dying. I suddenly realized how embarrassing this situation was. I eventually calmed down so that I could speak again.

"Ms. Jane has files on all of us," I said to them. "She has copies of our birth certificate and all of our records."

"Well, that makes sense," Jackson said. "She would want to know who she was bringing into her house."

"But how did she get them?" Chase asked.

"It doesn't matter how she got them," Kendall argued. "All that matters is that she is trying to protect us. She saved our lives, and now, she is taking care of us."

"Like Alex said, we don't know her intentions," said Chase. "We can't be sure of everything."

"She probably has them so she could know what kind of person we were or what family background we came from," Ash said.

"Agreed," Jackson said. Ash looked at him for a split second and turned away.

"But what if we didn't have a good background? Would she not have saved us? Would she have let us die?" Britt asked.

"Really! What would she have done then?" Chase backed up Britt.

"All we can judge Ms. Jones on are the kind things she has done for us," Kendall said.

"She did keep those files from us though," Henry said.

"So she did one thing that we could be a little skeptical about. Doesn't mean we have to turn against her now," Ash said.

"It's not like she trusts us," Chase said. "She doesn't tell us anything, and maybe, it's because she doesn't want us to know why she's really protecting us."

"She said she is trying to protect us." Ash was getting irritated with Chase.

"And Congress said they were going to take us to a better place. Are you really that naive?" You could tell what Chase said hurt her.

"She's not naive ; she just has a heart. Maybe you should try getting one." Jackson stood up for Ash. Chase wasn't expecting Jackson to defend Ash, but Ash was even more surprised.

"I'm talking to my girlfriend right now. That is none of your concern."

"Well, maybe you should learn how to treat her."

"The way I treat her has nothing to do with you." Chase walked towards Jackson.

"It does have to do with me if you're treating her badly. She's too good for you, and you know it."

"This little crush you have on my girlfriend has got to go. You don't know anything about us."

"I know the only reason you're with her is because Mimi never gave you a chance. You hoped that you could get over her by dating her best friend. She doesn't deserve that. She deserves a guy who cares for her and treats her with respect."

I couldn't believe what Jackson just said and neither could Chase. I could see Chase clutch his fist. He raised his arm, but Josh pulled him back while Henry moved Jackson out of the way.

"Okay," Josh said, "well I guess this wouldn't be the best time to say we unlocked the door."

It was a small closet. There were no clothes. Instead, there was a computer on the floor.

"What's in it?" Britt was excited.

"It looks like a laptop and a controller," Henry said.

"The controller only has one button," Josh said.

"That's really strange. Should we push it?" I asked. If Ms. Jane kept a closet locked that only contained a key and a controller, then the controller had to give us information. "What about the laptop?" Britt asked.

"I will try and hack into it." Henry took the laptop and sat at the desk. I knew Henry was smart, but it seemed like he could do everything.

"So, is anyone going to push it?" asked Josh.

We were all afraid of what would happen if we pushed the remote.

"I'm not for sure if we should," Kendall said.

"If we want answers, we have to take risks…right?" Ash said.

"We still don't know if Ms. Jane can be trusted," said Chase. "What if this button makes people aware of our location?"

"I highly doubt Ms. Jane would do that to us," Ash said.

"Remember why we're here guys. We wanted more information on Team Life. If she is a part of that program then we should not question her morality anymore."

Britt ran up and grabbed the remote.

"I can't handle it anymore." She pushed the button. All of a sudden, the wall in the front of the room opens up. A flat-screen TV comes up.

"She was hiding a TV?" Britt looked disappointed.

"Maybe we can watch the news on here," Josh said.

"Then where is the actual remote?" Britt asked.

"Just push the buttons on the TV," Josh said.

I turned the TV on. There were two reporters: a woman and a man.

"This was a terrible, terrible idea, and then, they try to hide it from us," the woman said. She was speaking to another man.

"I understand the concept, but this is not American at all. America does not stand for murder. We stand for justice," the man said.

"Exactly. I agree with you completely. How could a law so corrupt be passed? Countries with a higher population rate have never tried anything like this."

"China did have the one-child policy. Their strategy has gotten better over the past years, and what they have is very similar to our situation in the states."

"Don't you think it would be more logical to have a law similar to that? It is unbelievable that this country would prey on lower class people, on lower class children. That is outrageous." The woman clenched her face in disgust. "Even the one-child policy is un-

American. Our form of government is a republic. This should be outlawed. As Americans, we value freedom and independence. This is unconstitutional. How could the judicial branch let this be passed?"

While the two reporters. discussed the law, they showed videos of people protesting around the country. Large crowds of people were holding up signs saying "Let Them Live" and "Don't Kill Another Innocent Life.

"People are protesting. You can see that our citizens are upset with our government. We need people to continue doing something about this so something can change."

"Eufaula, Alabama, was not the only place that had an entire camp of children be saved. There are others in Arkansas, Tennessee, Kentucky, and other states. We will elaborate more right after this break," the woman finished.

"So people are fighting for us," I said. "People are protecting us." Relief was all I felt. Maybe we were safe. Maybe this would end soon. "Ms. Jane is trying to protect us," Ash said. "She can be trusted."

"It did not say anything about Team Life guys," said Chase. "If there are so many followers, then why are we still in hiding? This just lets us know we have people on our side. I am pretty sure there are news channels supporting the government."

"How can you be so negative?" asked Kendall.

"I'm being realistic." Chase was right. Ms. Jane would have the television kept on a news channel that rejected the law, not supported it.

"I understand what Chase is saying though. It's nice to know that we do have people supporting us, but there are probably just as many people supporting the government. This still doesn't give us that much information on Team Life," I said. All of a sudden, the television screen turned black.

"The screen on the Laptop is black too," Henry said.

"Oh my gosh! What did you do?" Britt started freaking out. The TV showed a girl sitting down with a huge smile on her face.

"Oh my gosh! I got someone. Brianna, Cesar, Brandon, everyone come in here!" said the girl.

"Hello, who is this?" Britt asked. She was too excited to listen to Britt. She looked about my age. It didn't make sense for Ms. Jane to be in contact with people our age. "My name is Layla. We are other survivors." Other people began walking into the room.

"What is this?" Britt asked. "Who are you guys?"

"This is what Team Life uses to contact each other," Layla said. "We are a group of kids that one of the members of Team Life saved. We found out how they contacted each other a week ago, and ever since, we hoped that another group of kids would hack into their laptop and figure it out."

Another girl looked exactly like Layla walked into the screen. "This is my twin, Ariana." She was not as energetic as Layla. She seemed much more reserved.

"So your member of Team life is keeping you guys in the dark too?" Josh asked.

"Team Life's policy is to protect us," Ariana said. "They believe the best way to do that is to not tell us what is going on. Even though a civil war is arising."

"What!" we all yelled.

"Not literally. It's nothing like the confederacy and union. So many people are protesting for and against the law. Neighbors, co-workers, and spouses—they're all turning against each other. These protests are splitting the country in half, not geographically, but socially. Team Life is trying to prevent that."

Suddenly, one of the guys said: "I'm Brandon by the way."

They all looked so excited to see someone else.

"How?" I looked into the screen and asked.

"The members of Team Life are powerful people from all over the nation," said Ariana. "If anyone can truly stop this war from happening, it's them," she said. "There are hundreds of people apart of this group."

I was blown away by how much information they obtained with such little help from their leader.

"How are they not getting caught? Can't this computer be traced?" Henry asked.

"One of the members created this software that the government can't trace. It's genius, I know." There was so much hope in her voice.

"So what's Team Life's strategy?" asked Henry.

"I know they're planning on hurting the economy to threaten the government," said one of the guys. "I think starting Sunday, they are going on a strike. No driving, no work, no grocery shopping ;they're not doing anything for a week."

"That doesn't sound that effective," I said.

"You don't understand how big Team Life is," laughed out one of the kids. "There may be hundreds of Team Life members, but there are millions of followers. That will hurt the economy tremendously."

"Actually," said Britt, "that sounds great."

"Guys, Mr. Haun is back!" one of the kids yelled.

"We have to go!" said Layla worriedly.

"Wait," I said, "there is so much more you guys have to tell us."

"Guys, we have to go! I am so sorry but get back on tomorrow at noon, and we will tell you everything you need to know! It was so nice meeting you guys."

One of the guys yelled at Layla to hurry up. "We got to go bye!" They were gone.

"Wow," Ash said.

"I know," Kendall said.

"That was incredible," I said. I didn't know what to call it. There so much we didn't know and so much they knew. There was so much Ms. Jane was keeping from us. It was relieving to know that there were others out there in the same position we were in. The passion in all of their voices compelled me to believe that something good would come out of this. That soon I wouldn't have to force myself to remember the sound of my mother's voice. That soon she would be placing ramen noodles in the microwave and calling it a home cooked meal. They spread an essential sense that I hadn't been able to feel since we were first saved. We all needed hope.

"Do we tell Ms. Jane we know?" Josh asked. That might have been the dumbest question he had ever asked.

"No!" everyone else yelled at him.

"Are you insane?" Britt hit him across the head.

"Why would we tell her? The other kids didn't tell," Chase said.

"Well, Ms. Jane can be easily persuaded into doing what we want her to. We might get even more information." Josh defended himself.

"Then what would the Team Life members think about that?" I said. "We can't tell Ms Jane. I don't even know if we should tell Alex right now. We have to keep this to ourselves. Agreed?"

"Agreed."

Chapter 5

"So what did you guys do today?" Ms. Jane asked us at the dinner table.

"Oh, nothing!" Josh said. "We just watched movies and played games all day! Nothing interesting!"

Britt nudged him.

"That's good. I hope you guys like the Chinese tonight." I felt horrible lying to Ms. Jane. She was so kind. After speaking with the other fugitives, I knew we all could trust her. She was only trying to help us. I wish Alex understood that.

"I love Chinese food!" I told her. "It's my favorite."

"The food is delicious," Britt said. Everyone else nodded. There was an awkward aura that spread across the dinner table. We now knew what was going on, but she was unaware of that. With Ms. Jane's unpredictable character, there was no telling how she would react to what we did. It was important for us to not say or do anything that would make her suspicious of us, just as it was important for her not to tell us.

"I'm glad you guys are enjoying it." She smiled. She started to look around. "Where is Alex?"

I didn't know where he went. I hadn't seen him since he had yelled at me earlier.

"He is not feeling well," said Kendall, "so he is just lying in his bed."

"Oh, dear. I will go check on him." That was not a good idea. Ms. Jane started to get up from the table.

"No," Kendall said. "I don't know if you would enjoy that." She turned towards me. "I just talked to him, and he doesn't want to see anyone."

I ignored Kendall.

"Oh well, I hope he feels better." Ms. Jane seemed concerned. I wish Alex knew how much she cared. His anger was directed towards his family, not Ms. Jane. We continued to eat dinner in silence. No one knew what to say, not even Britt—and she always knew what to say. So many things had happened in one day, and it was almost too much to handle. I stood up and left the table. I didn't know what hit me, but I had to leave that kitchen.

"I'm sorry, but I'm really tired. Thank you so much, Ms. Jane." I smiled and walked to the staircase. I passed Alex's room. Part of me wanted to go in and talk to him, but the other didn't think he deserved my kindness. I just wanted to be his friend. That was all I wanted to do for him, and he didn't let me. Now, I didn't want to waste my time concerning myself with him when he was just going to push me out. One day we would be close, but by the next day we would be fighting. It was a constant struggle with him. I cared about him, and I wanted to be there for him, but I no longer believed that we could ever be friends. It would never be the way we were on the trails. That was a faint memory that I desperately wanted to relive. I couldn't continue hoping that my past would become my present again. I went to my room and stared at the ceiling, trying to figure out what I felt.

"Mimi!" It was Britt, Ash, and Liz. "Are you okay?" Liz asked.

"I am fine," I said. I didn't know what I was feeling, but fine seemed like the best answer even with everything that had happened today. It was like Pandora's box had just opened, leaving a little hope behind.

"Oh man," Britt said, "was today crazy or what?" She walked to my bed and jumped on it.

"Tell me about it," Ash said. Today was a pretty hectic day for Ashley. "So what are you going to do about the whole Chase-and-Jackson situation?" I asked Ash.

"I don't know what to do. I'm so confused. Jackson and I barely talk, and out of the blue, he decides to stand up for me against Chase." It was somewhat random for Jackson to admit to liking Ash. He never mentioned her when we talked. Maybe she was the reason he started talking to me. I thought I had found a friend.

"How do you feel about the things Jackson said about Chase?" Liz asked. "Do you think they were true?"

Ash remained quiet.

"Are you referring to him saying that Chase only used Ash to get over Mimi?" Britt said. Britt always had to be so blunt. I didn't know how to react to that. I loved Ash, and she was my friend. I didn't care for Chase at all.

"Yes, Brittney," Liz said. "Didn't we already have a conversation about how blunt you are? Tone it down."

"Sorry, guys," Britt said.

"I guess part of me always knew that he liked you," Ash said. "I just liked the fact that someone gave me attention."

"Ash, you are gorgeous," said Britt. You don't need a guy to make you feel special. You already are."

"Seriously," I agreed.

"The way Jackson stood up for you was incredible," Britt said. "I'm totally Team Jackson all the way." We laughed. It was nice to be able to laugh about something that happened today. "I don't know him," Ash said.

"Well," said Liz, "get to know him."

"Wait, so does this mean you and Chase aren't together anymore?" I asked. Ash thought about it.

"Ash, you better say yes," Britt said. "I didn't really like him anyways. He is not good for you. Jackson is!"

"I have to agree with Britt," said Liz. "You and Chase are completely different. You and Jackson had similar ideas about Ms. Jane so you guys have more in common." She had a point.

"We agreed on one thing," said Ash. "That means nothing, and agreeing on everything isn't necessarily a good quality to have in a relationship."

"Jackson, Jackson, Jackson." Britt chanted his name as if she was at a game cheering for a team. It was nice to have moments like this. With so much chaos going around, I still had my friends.

"I can't believe there are hundreds of other survivors," said Britt. "Is that not awesome?"

"I know!" exclaimed Liz. "We weren't the only ones who escaped. This whole time I have been thinking the worst possible things."

I assumed that other people tried to escape like we did—but not everyone survived.

"People have died though," I said, "children, teens, maybe even people we knew at school but never talked to, or acquaintances."

"Let's not think about that right now," Ash said.

"You sound like Alex," I said. Alex never wanted to talk about death.

"What exactly happened?" Britt asked. "He became a completely different person when he found out about the files. One moment, I see you hugging him, and the next, I hear him yelling at you on the staircase!"

"There was information on his files that he didn't know about. It had to do with his biological parents. It just freaked him out, and he got upset."

"He still shouldn't have talked to you like that," Ash said. I didn't think it was right for him to say those things to me, but I knew he didn't mean them.

"Ash, he was upset. At that time, he didn't want to hear what anyone had to say. He was thinking irrationally, and I'm pretty sure he has calmed down now. I just know that he didn't mean those things."

"So what are you going to do?" asked Liz. "Go talk to him and forgive him like you always do?"

"He's never been an actual jerk to me in the past. This was the only time."

"Mimi, he is always a jerk to you." Ash agreed with Liz.

"I don't think he is. I think Alex is pretty cool." Surprisingly, Britt was on my side.

"Why do you have a problem with him?" I asked Ash and Liz. I never knew that Ash didn't like Alex, and I thought Liz did. I knew Ash didn't like the fact that I liked him because he was older than me, but it sounded like she didn't like him initially. She was just pretending.

"I just don't think he is someone you should like as more than a friend. He is not good for you Mimi," Ash said.

"I agree one hundred percent," Liz said.

"So because of his age, he is a terrible person to you?" This was really bothering me. Not once had I ever heard Ashley say she didn't like him, and all of a sudden, she was acting like it was a sin for me to be friends with him.

"I never said anything about his age," she said. "I just think he is a terrible person for you. You shouldn't like him." I could not believe what Ash was saying.

"Well, unfortunately, you can't control who you like. It's not like I'm acting on it. We are just friends. That's it." I understood the age difference between Alex and me. We were three years apart. He would be going to college, and I would be going to my sophomore year of high school, but I couldn't control my feelings. The more I tried not to like him, the more I liked him. It was impossible for you to choose who you like.

"You still need to at least try to move on," Ash said.

"I already hide my feelings from him. I can't force myself to not like him, and I refuse to waste my time trying. I understand what you are getting at, but I'm not doing anything wrong. If liking a guy three years older than me is bad then kill me—" Britt interrupted me.

"Speaking of death. We have a much greater problem on our hands. Oh yeah, people actually trying to kill us!" yelled Britt.

"I said I don't want to talk about that," Ash said,

"Well, it is more important than talking about Mimi's feeling for Alex," imposed Britt. Ashley shrugged.

"We will get more information tomorrow. What else is there to talk about?"

For some reason, Ash did not want to talk about it. She was always concerned and wanting to debate.

"What is wrong with you Ash?" I asked.

"Nothing."

She was hesitant. Ash was always the person that had it under control. She never cracked under pressure. "Are you sure?" I asked her. "We can talk about it."

"It's nothing, really," she said. "Britt, what did you want to say?"

"No!" said Britt. "I want to know what is wrong with you! You are never like this." It was clear that Ash did not want to talk about what was bothering her and Britt did not know how to handle those situations. She was the type of person that would demand it out of you because she cared so much. Her heart was in a good place, but sometimes, the way she went about things were not always in the most certified ways.

"She obviously doesn't want to talk about it. Back off," attributed Liz.

"She is my best friend, and I am concerned!" Britt gave Liz a death stare. I knew what she was thinking. Liz had barely known Ash, and she thought Liz was out of place, but Britt was more worried about Ash. She looked back at Ash. "What's wrong?" she asked more calmly.

"I really don't want to talk about it," Ash said. Britt was taken back. She was used to getting what she wanted—even if it was a friend's issues.

"All right, I understand." Unexpectedly, Britt respected her decision. Usually, Britt would continue to hassle, but she didn't. "If you don't want to tell me right now, that's fine. I want to know that I am always here though," said Britt. Ash smiled. Everything was quiet for a good minute until someone started banging on the door.

"Who is it?" I yelled.

"Josh."

"Open the door," Britt yelled. Josh came in.

"Did you forget?" he asked.

"Forget what?" Britt said.

"After dinner, we have a meeting. You decided this yesterday," Josh said.

Britt was alarmed. "Oh yeah! Has everyone been waiting on me?"

"No. People were about to go to bed, but I reminded them."

"Thanks, Josh! You are a lifesaver!" She ran up to him and kissed him on the cheek. She turned to us." Okay guys let's go!"

"I don't really feel like it," I said.

"Agreed," said Ash and Liz at the same time.

"Well, too bad! Get up and come on. It will be a short meeting, I promise." Britt was still demanding, but we all listened and followed her anyways. I went to the kitchen, and Kendall, Jackson, Henry, and Jason were the only people there.

"Where is everyone?" Britt was disappointed.

"Alex is still in his room. He says that he won't be able to go to the meeting today. He isn't feeling that great." Kendall smirked at me. She thought she was better than me because Alex was talking to her. I could tell by her snarky attitude.

"Chase is not exactly in the mood to see Jackson," said Henry.

"Actually, we forced Chase not to go. We all knew he was going to try and kill Jackson, so we kept him in Alex's room," Josh told Britt. Jackson was expressionless. The fact that someone wanted to fumble his face into the ground didn't faze him. He couldn't care less.

"Oh well, that is unfortunate." She was still disappointed. "Well, thank you all for coming. It means a lot to me," said Britt. "Now we have gotten a lot of new information today, and we will learn even more tomorrow, but does anyone have any questions on what we already know?" No one said anything. "Anyone?"

Kendall raised her hand. "We told the kids we would tell them if we found out any more information. Are we going to or not?"

"Well, what do you guys think we should do?" Britt asked.

"I don't think we should," Liz said. "It will scare them."

"They already know people are trying to kill them," said Henry. "If they are fine with knowing that, then telling them there are other survivors, if anything, should comfort them."

"I agree with Henry," Josh said. "We keep treating them like they are five, but in reality, they're in middle school. They are not as young as we treat them."

"I think we should tell them," I said.

"They really don't need to know," argued Liz.

"Majority rules," Britt said, "so we are telling them."

"I agree with Liz," whispered Jason. He was so quiet. It was probably the second time I had ever heard that kid talk.

"Well, two out of eight. Majority still rules." Britt smiled. "Any other questions?"

"Chase did have a point," Josh said. "I know Ms. Jane is a part of Team life, but how do we know that this is not just out of her best interest. This could be a game she is playing to raise her current status or something."

"Who cares if she is helping us so she can benefit from it later? She is still helping us," said Kendall.

"Her actions may be good, but her intentions may not be," Jackson said to her,

"She has given us no reason to think otherwise," replied Kendall.

"Ms. Jane has been kind to us," Henry said. "Until we have evidence that she is untrustworthy, we will figure out what to do then. Let's leave that alone until we cross that bridge."

"Henry is right," said Britt. "When she gives us proof that she can't be trusted, then we can decide what to do with her. Until then, let's all go to sleep and find out more information tomorrow. Meeting adjourned," She said while hitting her fist on the kitchen table. We all left and went to our rooms. After such a long day, we all needed rest.

Chapter 6

I woke up excited to talk to the other survivors, it was itching me all day. There was nothing else to be excited about. Alex was still being...Alex. He would not talk to me or even look at me the one time he came downstairs. Ash and I were not on the best of terms right now either. We had one conversation with Britt, but it was not the same. She spent time with Jackson that morning though. Chase looked angry and tried talking to me, but I blew him off. Britt was spending more time with Henry. I didn't really understand their relationship—I didn't even think Henry did. He spoke with her, but he still would seem a little confused each time she interacted with him. Josh didn't seem to mind. I didn't really understand what Britt was doing, but it was Britt. No one ever understood her. Kendall continued to talk about how Alex would not be coming downstairs because he was sick and didn't want to talk to anyone. She would always give me a giant smirk when she would say anything about him. She thought she was getting under my skin, but I just ignored her every time. I was not going to give her the satisfaction.

"So you said you will tell us if you found out anything?" asked John. "Did you?" John, Andrew, Ash, Britt, and I were in the kitchen.

"The truth is…" Ash could not finish her sentence.

"The truth is that we did not find anything," Britt said. "There was a locked door in the office, but we could not unlock it. Such a shame." She smiled and walked upstairs.

"I know you're lying!" said Andrew.

"It's complicated." Ash did not want to tell them.

"Yesterday, you said you understood us. You promised you would tell us." John was upset.

"We found out that there are people trying to protect us," I told them. "We were able to watch a news channel and see people arguing about the situation we are in. There were people protesting for us, and Ms. Jane is one of the people trying to help us. She can be trusted." Ash mouthed thank you.

"That is great news! Does that mean we'll be out soon?" John asked.

"We are not sure about that," Ash said.

"Well, that's fine with me. That means I get to spend more time with you!" Andrew winked.

"Maybe you should find a girl your age," I said.

"They're too immature," said Andrew, "I need a real woman to be by my side." He put his arm around Ash's shoulder.

"And that is my cue to leave." I walked upstairs. Ash followed.

"Mimi," said Ash, "I am sorry about last night. It was uncalled for."

"We don't have to talk about it, remember?" I opened the door to my room, and Chase was there. "What are you doing?" He was always showing up in my room randomly, but I figured this had nothing to do with me.

"Ash," he said, "can I speak to you."

"Sure." She walked towards him. Chase looked at me.

"Alone."

"Oh! Okay, I will leave." I closed the door and stood by it to see if I could listen. It was really hard to listen. There was a ton of mumbling, and nothing was really clear.

"We need to talk," Chase said.

"You already made that clear. What do you want?" Ash said with an attitude. She hardly ever expressed irritation.

"I want to know what is going on between you and Jackson?"

"I barley know him."

"You've been spending more time with him, and the way he talked about you yesterday right in front of me was unacceptable. I don't think it's a good idea to talk to him." I could not believe he just said that. The way he treats Ash was rude. He was rude to her, and everything Jackson said was true.

"Excuse me?"

"I don't want you talking to him."

"I don't think you have the right to choose who I talk to. I control that."

"Why do you want to be friends with him? He's a tool. Do you like him or something, because if you do, then we can end this right now."

"So is that what you came here to do? End our relationship? Obviously," Ash said, but I couldn't hear her anymore. All I could hear were the footsteps coming my way.

"Mimi, what are you doing?" Jackson asked.

I didn't know if I should have told him or not, but I did anyway. I whispered,

"Listening to Ash and Chase fight about you! Now be quiet!"

"What!" he said and got down right beside me and started listening to their conversation.

"Do you agree with what he said? Do you think I treat you bad because I feel like I have been kind to you this entire time?" Chase started to yell. It became much easier to hear now.

"What about what he said about Mimi?" Oh, goodness. "Was all of that true? We all know that you liked her before you and I were together. That was apparent." He got quiet. "Exactly."

"That is beside the point."

"That is the point, Chase. You never liked me. You liked Mimi. Jackson was right. You can't even deny it."

"What's going on here?" Liz asked.

"Hush!" Jackson and I both said.

"Who is in our room, Mimi?"

"Shut up and find out!" Jackson said. She did exactly that.

The fight continued: "This is about Jackson. You have feelings for him! Just admit it! You have ever since we have been stuck in this house. I have seen the way you both look at each other. Do not try and make this about me and Mimi!"

"What's all the noise?" Kendall asked. She was with Alex. This whole time I thought she was lying about talking to him—she was actually telling the truth. He confided in her and not me. I did not understand why. She was obnoxious. I couldn't believe it. I looked the other and put my left ear near the door. I was facing Jackson. He understood my facial expression.

"Shut up and listen," he said. Kendall was behind Jackson. She stood up and put her ear next to the door. Alex bent over beside me put his right ear by the door facing me. He made no eye contact with me. I turned the other way.

"For goodness sake, I barely know Jackson, but he has treated me better than you ever have. You have never said anything like he said about me yesterday!"

"Stop playing a victim! I have never been mean to you. I have never treated you poorly. Stop pretending like I have. What do you want Ashley, attention? You cannot give me one time I have treated you badly. All you want is attention! Are you jealous of Mimi or something? It is starting to seem that way." Then I heard a smack.

"How dare you say you have never treating me poorly and say the things you just said to me? If you ever really cared about me, then you wouldn't have the audacity to even say something like that." I could tell she was crying. "You say I'm pretending. Why don't you stop pretending like you don't like Mimi? Just finally admit that you like her. You never liked me."

"I don't like Mimi!".

"No! You won't admit it because we all know that there is only one guy in this house that Mimi cares about more than anyone, and it is not you. I am so thankful that it is not you because she deserves better, and he is twenty times better than you. You can continue thinking that you deserve her, but you don't. He does."

"Hey, Ash. Wait a minute."

"Let go of me!"

Right after she screamed, Jackson got up, which pushed Kendall down, and opened the door. He stormed towards Chase and pushed him.

"Don't put your hands on her!" shouted Jackson.

"We were having a private conversation, once again!" Chase swung at Jackson but missed. Jackson pushed him down.

"Stop! Stop!" yelled Ash. Jackson looked at Ash and listened to her. Britt and Henry ran to the door.

"What the hell is going on?" Henry asked.

"They got in a fight over Ash," Kendall said. I hate her. Britt ran over to Ash and hugged her. She was still crying.

"If you ever make her cry again I swear I—" Jackson started but was cut off.

"Oh, shut up! You're not her boyfriend. She doesn't want you. Just get out," said Chase.

"No, you get out!" I said. "We all heard what you said to her. If you even think for a second that Ash still wants you, then you are kidding yourself. Get out!" I yelled.

"No offense, but as I told Jackson, it is none of your business."

"Get out of my room!" I started moving toward him. I thought I was going to completely tackle him down, but Alex held me back. "Get off me! Don't touch me!" He let go. I looked at Chase, still in my room, and I was about to run after him again, but this time Henry grabbed me.

"I think you need to calm down, Mimi," Henry said.

"He is right," Britt said. "But seriously, Chase, get out." He didn't move. He was about to say something, but Ash interrupted him.

"Get out!" Ash said. He looked at her with grief and walked out.

"Are you okay?" Jackson asked. The sincerity in his voice could not be replicated. Watching Jackson made me certain that Chase never cared for Ash. Ash didn't say anything, but I think it was better that she couldn't. She couldn't answer that question.

"I think," said Britt, "maybe you should go too, Jackson," He respected her opinion and started to walk out.

"Wait!" Ash said. He turned around, and she hugged him. "Thank you." She stood there crying on his shirt for about a minute.

"Well, guys," said Henry, "it is almost noon, so I will go get everyone in the office. Y'all do not have to come if you don't feel like it." Henry was concerned. He was such a respectful person.

"We might go. You can start without us," Britt told Henry.

"Okay." He turned to Alex. "Are you coming?"

"I don't know. I might just go back to my room." He walked off.

"I will go with you!" Kendall said excitedly.

"No, it's fine. I would rather be alone," he said calmly.

"Oh, okay. I'll come up there in an hour and tell you all about it."

"No, that's fine too. I want to be alone."

"Okay."

I could tell she was upset. I couldn't help but feel bad for her. Being rejected by Alex was not the best feeling in the world. He walked off while she walked away with Henry. Ash let go of Jackson. She wasn't crying anymore.

"Will you be okay?" Jackson asked.

"I will be." She smiled.

"I will see you later." He walked away. Ash shut the door.

"So I would like to know what all happened?" Britt asked.

"It is a long story, and I do not feel like reliving that," said Ash.

"Mimi? Liz?"

"Hey, I didn't start listening till the middle of it," Liz said.

"They got into a fight about Jackson, and he accused her of liking Jackson and wanting attention and being jealous of me," I told Britt. "Then," I said to Ash, "I'm guessing he grabbed your hand when you told him not to touch you. After that, Jackson barged in and pushed Chase."

"This is why I was Team Jackson. I knew Chase was no good. How are you feeling Ash?" Britt asked.

"Better."

"Is that how he was the entire relationship? Was he always a jerk?" Britt continued.

"He was at times because he wanted Mimi and couldn't have her. He was right though—he was not always mean. He did not always treat my terribly, he just did not like me the way he likes you." I didn't know what to say to that. "Besides, I know Jackson cares a lot. He treats me so differently than Chase did, and it isn't because Chase was a bad guy, it is because Jackson truly likes me. I know right now you all feel obligated to hate Chase, but please don't. We both said things we did not necessarily mean."

"That will be hard to do," Britt said. "I hate him."

"You may say that he wasn't always a jerk to you, but he was today!" I said. "I don't like him."

"By the way, Mimi, I'm sorry for mentioning Alex while you guys were listening. I wasn't sure if y'all were, so I tried to be careful with my words.

"Ha! That was not a problem. You didn't say his name, and honestly, I don't really know how I feel about him right now. Thank you for saying what you did about him. I thought you hated him."

"Wait! She said nice things about Alex?" Britt said. "I wish I was there so badly."

"I couldn't believe what she said about Alex either!" Liz said. Britt and Liz laughed.

"It was the truth, Mimi. He is good for you. I was just a little jealous last night. I tried to make up for it in the argument with Chase."

"Jealous of me? I like a guy who shows no interest in me. There is nothing to be jealous about, and you, most definitely, made up for it."

"You may feel that way, but he does care about you. You don't realize it right now, but eventually, you will."

"All right," I said, "we will see about that."

"We can go to the meeting if you want," said Ash.

"Are you sure you want to?" Britt asked.

"I'm great right now."

"Okay, well then, let's go."

We walked downstairs and into Ms. Jane's office. Everyone, except Alex and Chase, were in there looking at the screen. Then I spotted John and Andrew. I figured Henry would go ahead and tell them everything we knew. Although he was much older than them, he did not view them as children. He understood that they were going through this just like we were and had a right to know what was going on.

"What are they doing in here?" Of course Liz didn't approve.

"Let's just listen," I said. We walked in front of the screen.

"Oh good! I remember you!" said someone from the screen. It was either Ariana or Layla, but by the enthusiasm in their voice, I could tell it was Layla.

"Okay, so this is what we know," Cesar said. "They are starting the strike tomorrow. This means that we will not be able to communicate with each other till next week. We pretty much told you everything we knew yesterday. There are a ton of followers and members trying to protect us. This is the first major move since they kidnapped us. It hopefully will work, but we do not know for sure. Neither do the members."

"Do you have any extra information to share with us?" The guy I believed to be Brandon asked.

"No," Britt said. "We have not been told anything or have been able to find anything in her office. I think she keeps most of her information at work."

"It has been hard finding information for us too," said one of the twins.

"What happens if this strike doesn't work?" Josh asked.

"We honestly don't know. Anything could happen. We might be stuck here even longer."

"Do you know where our families are?"

"Many parents are in jail for going against the government's wishes. Others might be living normal lives. We are really not sure, but we do know that Team Life members have spoken with everyone's parents and told them that you are safe."

"So our parents know where we are? That is great!" I said. I was glad to know that my mother was not worried sick about me. She did not need to be. I was safer than she knew.

"We have to go again! Mr. Haun always randomly comes to check up on us! He is in the garage! Bye!" Brandon said, and then, they were gone.

"Our parents know we are safe!" Andrew said.

"I miss them so much," John said.

"Yes, yes, we all do!" Britt said. "Well, you got to listen in on one of our meeting. Yay! Congrats. Now, you can leave."

"Brittney!" Liz, Ash, and I yelled.

"What?"

"Be nice."

She stayed quiet.

"So this explains why she had our files. She had to contact our parents," Josh said.

"Maybe, Alex can get over this file thing now," Kendall said.

"It isn't just the fact that she had his files, Kendall," I said, "it is about what was on them. Since you guys are so close now, I thought you would know that."

"Someone seems a little jealous." She smirked.

"I've noticed how much you have tried to rub it in my face. I don't really care. I do not have to follow him everywhere just to get him to pay attention to me. He is my friend."

"Really? So did I just dream him yelling at you on the staircase about how you don't know him at all? No, that actuality happened."

I hate her.

"Okay," Henry said, "we do not need another fight today. That is over."

"Seriously, guys," Britt said, "let's just get prepared for tomorrow. Ms. Jane will be here all of next week. If she sees us fighting, then she will be upset."

"You are right Brittney," said Kendall. "You know, I will just go and tell Alex that." She looked at me. "He really needs someone to talk to right now. Maybe if he knows about the files, he will be better."

"I could have sworn he told you to leave him alone," I said to her.

She pretended like she didn't hear me and walked off.

"You know," Britt said, "I used to like that girl."

"She is just frustrated with Alex right now," Jackson said, "Sometimes, she takes her anger out on other people."

"And why does that give her the right to treat me like complete crap?" I said.

"It doesn't. That is just how she is."

"She tries to rub it in Mimi's face that she is close to Alex when she really isn't," argued Britt.

"They are friends. They are together all the time," said Henry. He was not helping at all.

"That doesn't mean she has to be so foul toward Mimi. She knows how Mimi feels about Alex, and she takes advantage of her all the time."

"Britt!" I yelled.

"Sorry," she said, "but everyone knows, Mimi."

"Wait, you like Alex? That's why you don't like me? It all makes sense now," said Andrew.

"Great, now this kid is going to tell everyone." I did not need another person knowing.

"Don't tell anyone, Andrew!" Britt always had my back.

"I won't. As long as you give me a kiss."

Britt pulled Andrews arm back. "Ow Ow!"

"You won't tell anyone, right?"

"No, I won't! I promise! Please stop! Ow!"

She let go. He ran into the playroom.

"I actually praise your callousness right now," Ash said. " That was awesome!"

"Whatever," said Britt. "You'll be changing your mind tomorrow."

"We all love you, Britt!" I said. She ignored us.

"Okay, guys! Well, we have a long week ahead of us. Let's make the best of it," Britt said. "Meeting adjourned!" That was her favorite phrase now. We weren't even in a meeting.

Chapter 7

The week began slowly. Ms. Jane announced that she would not have work for an entire week. They were on vacation. We all pretended like we believed her even though we knew she was lying. It was not that different having Ms. Jane at home. Sometimes she would play with the younger children, but the majority of the time, she was in her office. She rarely came out. Since she was home, many people changed their attitudes. There were no major fights between anyone. Kendall continued on following Alex everywhere. Chase and Ash were not talking, and thank goodness, Jackson and Chase were not fighting either. Things were pretty boring. I woke up, ate, went to my room, left my room to eat again, went back to my room, and then slept. However, Jackson and Ash were interesting to watch. Whenever they saw each other, they would smile. Jackson would always have this concerned look on his face that would eventually turn into anger if and when Chase would pass by. Ash would have the most innocent facial expressions when she saw him. She didn't know what to do about the situation. Them two were not the only interesting things that were going on during the week. Britt and Henry still continued to confuse me. They started to become closer friends. She spent a lot of her time bugging him but would stop whenever he seemed annoyed. Although she was annoying him, he enjoyed her company. She was not talking to Josh as much, but he still didn't seem to mind. He was the only person that would talk to Chase after the fight the week before.

Our meetings did not continue during the week. People were so preoccupied with other things. Surprisingly, Britt did not care. She always tried to take charge in the meetings, but for some reason, she didn't want to have them. I guess there was nothing to talk about until the week was over. Since no one would be at the meetings, most people would hang out and play games in the game room. Kendall would still follow Alex to his room. He still would not leave his room, and he still would not talk to me. Alex was probably the most complicated person I knew. I would hardly ever see him, and when I did, he wouldn't make eye contact with me. I tried not to think about it, but with such an uneventful week, there was nothing else to do. "Mimi, what are you doing?" Liz asked me. We were in our room looking out the window.

"Thinking."

"About what?"

I did not respond. I was surprised she would even ask. "Never mind."

"I am so bored," I said. "This is seriously the most boring week of my life, and we still have a day left. Let this be over please." There was nothing to do, but then again, even when Ms. Jane was at work, there was still nothing to do in the house. We always had to do nothing but wait in her house.

"When is it not boring here? We are stuck in this house," Liz said.

"Still!"

"I'm pretty sure if you were talking to Alex you would not feel that way?" Liz just had to bring up Alex.

"Alex isn't talking to me right now."

"Then talk to him."

"Liz, you already know that he is mad at me."

"Oh please," she said, "he lets that girl follow him around everywhere and does not show an inch of irritation. We all know that she is irritating the crap out of him." Liz became so blunt.

"Maybe, he actually likes her." I always wondered if he did. People would always tell me he doesn't, but why would they tell me he did? He spent so much time with her. How could he not like her? It was inevitable.

"Oh my gosh, Mimi, stop feeling bad for yourself. Just talk to him."

"I will, eventually."

"Lies."

"Is not! One day, hopefully sooner than later, he will talk to me."

"Why do you have to wait for him to talk to you? It is bothering you more than it is bothering him."

"He is the one mad at me. He will talk to me in his own time."

"But you can talk to him now. This is not life and death here." Liz started to annoy me.

"I understand that." I walked away from the windowsill. Liz was irritating me. "I am leaving now."

"To talk to him?"

"To get a drink of water."

"You are pathetic."

I rolled my eyes. I walked out of the room, and as I closed the door, someone ran into me. I fell on my face. It had been a while since I had fallen. I wasn't nearly as clumsy as I was on the trail. I missed the rush before I hit the ground. Sometimes it was comfortable to lose total control of your body, and let gravity do everything for you, but only for a few seconds.

"Mimi? Are you okay? Sorry." A familiar voice said. I looked at his face. It was so serious. He bent over to grab my arms and pull me up, but I flinched.

"I'm fine." I got up.

"I really am sorry."

"It's fine." I started to walk away.

"I don't think it is," he said. I stopped and looked at him. It was the first time he made eye contact with me in days, and surprisingly, his eyes showed a hint of despair. It quickly disappeared as he looked away.

"Where's Kendall?" I never saw that girl leave his sight.

"I don't know. I don't own her."

"She seems to be attached to your hip these days.

"Are you jealous?" He made a slight smirk. He just had to smirk one time. That was all. His face quickly turned firm.

"That is exactly what I'm feeling, Alex. Congratulations for figuring that out," I said sarcastically. I walked off to go down the stairs.

"Wait."

I turned around.

"I really am sorry."

I knew he wasn't referring to running into me, but I decided to pretend like he was. "It didn't hurt that much. I got up didn't I?" I walked downstairs into the kitchen, and he followed me. John and Andrew were sitting at the kitchen table eating while playing a Nintendo DS. They were always playing video games.

"Hey!" I yelled, "You guys are not supposed to be playing video games at the kitchen table. Finish your food and play later," I said demandingly.

"Ms. Jane doesn't care if we play games," said Andrew. Usually, Alex would say something smart, but he didn't bother. He walked toward the refrigerator.

"Well, I do." I understood Britt's feeling of empowerment. It was a great feeling to contain.

"But—" John started to say something, but he was interrupted.

"It can wait," Alex said. Andrew glared at him. Alex noticed it. "It is just a video game, Andrew." Andrew continued to glare. "What?" said Alex.

"I don't like you," Andrew said.

"Why?"

Andrew didn't answer his question. He just looked at him and got up. He walked toward Alex. He put his middle and index finger up to his eyes.

"I will be watching you."

"Um, okay."

"You better treat her right." Andrew stepped on Alex's foot so hard Alex screamed. I tried my hardest not to laugh.

"Ow! What was that for?"

Andrew ran for it, and John followed. He did not want Alex to pound him into the ground. I didn't think that was on Alex's mind though. Alex turned and looked at me. "What was that about?" I shrugged. "Who was he even talking about? Kendall?" I shrugged again. I saw that John and Andrew left their plates at the table. I took their plates and walked toward the sink. Alex blocked my way. "You aren't talking to me."

I didn't know how to respond to that. I hope he wasn't trying to pretend like everything was okay because it wasn't. "I am not moving until you at least try to have a conversation with me."

"Alex, will you please get out of my way?" I said, but he leaned forward. His face was no less than an inch away from mine.

"Nope." He walked forward.

"What?" I couldn't look at those eyes again. "What do you want?" I asked politely. I stepped away. Being that close to him made me nervous.

"I want to talk to you. Is that too much to ask?" He got even closer towards me. All of a sudden there was a huge crack. The plate fell.

"Thanks, Alex." I bent down to pick up the pieces of glass.

"You were the one holding it."

"If you weren't in my way and getting so." I started. "Ugh, never mind." He leaned over to help me pick it up. "I got it!" I snapped.

"I was just trying to help."

"Well, I don't need your help." I grabbed the last piece of glass and threw it in the trash and walked out of the kitchen.

"Mimi."

"What do you want now?"

"You forgot the other plate." He was holding it in his hand. "I would put it in the sink, but since you said you didn't need my help, I am leaving it for you to do it—unless you need my help." I snatched it from him and put it in the sink. He still had the same smirk he always had. I walked back upstairs, acting as if I didn't want him to follow. He didn't. I secretly was hoping he would. I could not stay mad at him for long, no matter how angry he made me. These feelings were driving me insane. I went into my room, and Liz was still sitting at the same spot.

"So did you talk to him?" she asked.

"Kind of."

She turned around. Liz wasn't the type to get overly excited about something like Ash and Britt would, but it was obvious she was intrigued.

"About?"

'Nothing."

"So you didn't even bother to talk to him about anything? Nothing is resolved?"

"Um…not really." I got her point. It was a very pointless conversation, since I didn't bother to talk to him about anything.

"So what…are you guys just going to pretend like nothing happened so it can just happen again?"

"Hey! I was ignoring him. He was the one trying to talk to me. I didn't give him any of my attention."

"And that is supposed to make it better? You are being immature about this. Just talk to him Mimi." Liz was attacking me again. It was not a good day.

"Why do you care? Goodness. I will talk to him in my own time."

Liz looked frustrated.

"I am tired of you sitting around being sad. It is a downer to all of us."

I was not acting any kind of way. I was being the same me. "What are you talking about? I am the same Mimi."

"Everyone has been talking about you. You are usually a leader and try to plan stuff. Now, you listen to what goes on instead of partaking in it. You are not the same Mimi." Glad to know my friends were talking about me behind my back. "It isn't just since you and Alex got in a fight, it has been since we got here—when he first started ignoring you for Kendall. You expect him to come up to you all the time, and you do nothing. You just sit there and wait. Then get upset when nothing happens. That isn't how the world works, Mimi. You have to meet people halfway. So please, for the sake of our friendship and your other friendships, meet him halfway!"

I could not believe she just gave me a lecture. I guess she was a little right. I definitely could work on talking to Alex more.

"I guess you are right."

"Okay, well then go and talk to him now!"

"No! I just got done talking to him. I will do it soon, I promise."

She seemed to calm down a little.

"As long as you do it," she said, "Britt and Ash would be relieved."

Then I thought if Ash and Britt were complaining about me the same way Liz was.

"Wait a minute. Did they put you up to this?" Knowing Britt, she would want to be the main one telling me all of my flaws.

"No. They are planning on giving you an intervention tomorrow, but I couldn't wait."

That was comforting. "Well, I will make sure to tell them I am fine."

Someone opened the door. It was Britt, Henry, Ash, and Jackson.

"Hey guys, no intervention tomorrow. I am completely fine, and I will talk to Alex soon." They looked shocked.

"You told her Liz!" screamed Britt.

"Mimi, we can explain," Ash said.

"Seriously, Alex. Still," Jackson said.

"I thought you guys got over that today," Henry said. "He was going to talk to you."

"Wait, he talks about her?" Britt asked curiously. I could tell by the expression on Henry's face that he felt like he had made a mistake. He did not want to get caught in girl gossip and drama. "What did he say?" Britt was probably about to start a ramble of questions, but I made sure I stopped it.

"So where have you guys been? This is my first time seeing y'all all day!"

"It's only six," said Ash.

"Still."

"Sorry, Mimi. We were in the kitchen upstairs."

I forget that the little kids go to the kitchen down-stairs, and the rest of us eat on the third floor. I went to the one downstairs all the time.

"Oh, okay." I didn't know what else to say, but apparently, I was not being myself, so I needed to make sure I was myself. It got really quiet. It seriously felt like hours had passed, and we were so quiet.

"Hey guys! Let's play truth or dare," suggested Britt. That was such a juvenile game.

"Sure, why not," Henry said. I was surprised. He didn't seem like the type of person to play.

"Are you serious?" I asked.

"Yes. Mimi. Have a little fun, goodness."

I will admit that I felt pressured. "Fine," I caved.

"All right Britt, you first. truth or dare?" Liz asked.

"Truth."

Considering the fact that Britt was the one who wanted to play this game, I was so surprised that she went soft and chose truth.

"Why haven't you been hanging with Josh lately?"

Apparently, I wasn't the only one who noticed it. Liz did too.

She quickly answered: "He has been with Chase. He has no friends right now. Remember, everyone teamed up on him after…you know," said Britt.

"Are you defending him?" Ash said.

"Not at all! I still hate that guy. Team Ja…" She looked at Jackson. "Nevermind." I was proud of her. She was able to stop herself.

"Even before then, you weren't hanging out with him as much. Why?" Liz was asking all the questions I wanted to know the answers too.

"You only get one question and one answer," Britt said, "Okay, my turn." She looked around. "Mimi, truth or dare?" she asked. I didn't want to be a wimp.

"Dare."

She thought for a while.

"I dare you to go outside and stay out there for at least five minutes." I would, But we were forbidden to go outside.

"Britt, don't dare her to do that! We are fugitives! If someone sees her, then we all get caught." Ash spazzed out.

"Guys, it is dark outside. She will be fine," assured Britt.

"You don't have to do it if you don't want to," suggested Henry. I was not going to be afraid. Since everyone felt like I was not myself, why not be a little daring?

"I will."

Everyone was surprised.

"I actually was not expecting that," Britt said, "but okay." I got up and walked towards the door.

"Don't let anyone see you, Mimi. Please be safe." Ash was worried. She did not like the idea of this. Neither did I.

"No worries, guys. I will be fine." I opened the door and walked out. Something hit me and pushed me down. It was him again.

"Twice in less than a day," laughed Alex.

"I see there is no apology this time."

"Oh, my apologies." He smiled. He looked into the room and saw everyone sitting in a circle. "What are you guys doing?" he asked.

"Truth or dare," answered Britt. "Mimi has been dared to go outside and stay there for at least five minutes."

"That's stupid and dangerous. Don't do it." Alex grabbed my arm.

"It's a dare, and it's dark. Calm down."

"Are you insane? You're not going out there!" He had a tight grip around my arm. I tried to remove it, but he was too strong.

"Yes, I am now let go!" I shouted at him, but he didn't.

"I know you, Mimi. You will do something stupid and get caught."

I was annoyed at the insult. "You don't know me at all. You've been around me for what, a few months?" I referenced what he said to me earlier, and he knew that. He got quiet for a few seconds.

"You are not going out there."

"Just go with her Alex," suggested Liz.

"Oh yes! That way you can protect her." Britt grinned. I knew what they were up to.

"I will be fine," I said.

"I'm coming with you." He completely ignored me. He walked in front of me, still clutching my arm, but his hand slowly moved down to mine. He was holding my hand. We went downstairs.

"The backyard would be less visible," I suggested. He looked at the backyard and saw the back porch. There were at least three doors on the back wall, so you could just get inside the house. Alex tried every single one.

"They're locked." He searched for a key. I was surprised that he cared so much about a little dare.

"We could just use the front door. I'm sure the key is somewhere near the door."

"And risk you getting caught. I don't think so."

"You're so parental, goodness. I am not a little kid. You should stop treating me like one." I snatched my hand back.

"Well, maybe you should stop acting like one. I mean really, a dare."

"If it so foolish, then why are you participating in it?" I asked him. He was such a hypocrite. I knew for a fact he would be doing this at his house if we could.

"For you, Mimi. I am trying to keep you safe. Do you know how dangerous this is? This is not a joke, Mimi. If someone catches us, we're dead." He found the key. "Here it is." He unlocked the door, and we stood on the back porch.

"See," I said. "We are safe."

"Anything could happen." I looked at the window. Britt and Ash had moved into the kitchen. They were mouthing the words "Move out."

"Hey. I think Britt wants us to go into the actual backyard."

"No way."

"We can hide behind a tree. There are so many out here." I walked.

"Mimi, get back here."

"I am not Kendall who does everything you tell her to. So stop expecting me to do as you say." He followed me. I walked toward a tree. "We can hide here." I stood behind the tree. Alex stood behind, making sure no one could see us.

"Don't move." I could feel him breathing. We were standing behind a tree. There was no way anyone could see us.

"Hey!" said an unfamiliar voice. My heart skipped a beat.

"Follow me," said Alex. "Do not say anything."

"Hey," the voice repeated, "who is that there!"

Alex took my hand and grabbed me. We walked away from the tree. The voice was coming from a lady, possibly in her midthirties. She could see us now. Alex was right. Once someone saw us, we were dead.

Chapter 8

"Who is that?" the lady continued, "I have pepper spray!"

"Hello, Ma'am," said Alex. He smiled.

"Who are you, and what are you doing in Jane's backyard?" the lady asked sharply.

"I am the son of one of Ms. Jane's close friends," he said. "You probably don't know him. His name is Mathew." He couldn't come up with a better name. "He is out of town, so he let me stay at Ms. Jane's house for the weekend."

The lady continued to look suspicious. I couldn't tell if she was buying it or not.

"Who is that girl with you?"

"This is my girlfriend." My heart skipped a beat. "She thought it was so beautiful out here so we decided on going for a walk."

"Is that right?"

"Yes, Ma'am. You love it out here don't you?"

He told me not to say anything but I had to. "Yes! It is so beautiful," I said. "The flowers and trees are gorgeous. I have never seen such beautiful landscape. My house isn't nearly as pretty as Jane's."

"So you guys are not from around here?"

"No, Ma'am."

"Well, that was obvious when I saw y'all. You dress horrendously. For a while, I thought you guys were fugitives."

I froze. Alex laughed.

"No, Ma'am. We are certainly not." He flashed his charming smile.

"Well," she said, "let's ask Jane. Walk with me." She was not buying it. We walked to the front lawn. I didn't know what we were going to do.

"Do we really have to leave the landscape?" I looked at Alex. "It is so stunning. Look at the pool and the pond. We can stay for a little while longer, hunny."

"It's getting late, babe." He would use the term "babe." "I promise I will make it up to you."

"And how will you exactly?" I said.

"We can go and see that movie you have been dying to see for weeks."

"You have to do better than that." I smiled.

"How about I take you to the most expensive restaurant in this town?" He was really trying to sound romantic and completely failing at it.

"You can't buy my love, hunny. You know that." It was getting hard not to laugh.

"All right, well then, I will plan the most romantic night of your life tomorrow."

"And what will we do?" I asked.

"It's a surprise just for you." He winked and kissed me. It was short and quick. I didn't know what to do. I froze. I could barely breathe or even walk for that matter. Luckily, we were already at the door, so I didn't have to.

"We will see if your story is true, kids," the lady said in the snobbiest voice. She seemed like one of those self-absorbed, rich parents you see on television. She was everything Ms. Jane was not.

Ms. Jane opened the door and looked shocked for a quarter of a second, and then, her face went back to normal.

"Hey, Mrs. Wilson," Ms. Jane said. "So glad to see you! I see you met the kids."

"So they are yours. They told me this spurious story about how you are watching over them. I was about to turn them in."

"Oh goodness, no. That would have been terrible. They are definitely under my roof. No worries."

"I am so sorry, Jane. I didn't mean you any trouble." She turned and looked at us. "It was nice meeting y'all. Have a great night." The grin on her face was so large and fake. We never even told her our names. We walked in, and Ms. Jane closed the door behind us. I expected her to say something. She looked so disappointed.

"We can explain," I said.

"Sit down." Her voice was intimidating. We both did as she told us to. "Do you know what could have happened to you guys if she found out that you were a fugitive? What could have happened to everyone? Your actions were selfish and could have gotten all of us killed!"

"But we can explain," Britt said. I saw her, and everyone walk out of a closet. "It was my idea. I made her go outside."

"No, I chose to go out there on my own," I said.

"I do not care," said Ms. Jane. "I am disappointed in all of you. Don't you ever play a stunt like that ever again! Do you understand me?"

"Yes, Ma'am," we all said except Alex.

"Good," she said. "Now leave."

We all went upstairs after that. Alex let go of my hand and walked into his room.

"I am so sorry, Mimi," Britt said. "You could have been harmed."

"We were safe," I said.

"I understand if you are mad at me. You have every right to be," continued Britt.

"That lady was dumb. It's okay."

She stopped.

"So, what did you say to her?" Ash asked. I thought of the kiss.

"Nothing really. Alex just told her that Ms. Jane was taking care of us because her friend was out of town."

"She believed you guys were related?" Britt laughed. "That lady was stupid. You guys look nothing alike."

"Well, he didn't say we were siblings. He said we were a couple." I still couldn't believe he kissed me. I didn't know what to think of it, or even, if I should be thinking about it.

"Wait, so is that why you were holding hands when you walked in?" asked Ash.

"I guess."

"So you guys made up?" Liz asked.

"Um, I don't know," I said. "I guess we did."

He kissed me and left without saying anything to me. I didn't know what to think of that. He can't just kiss me and not say anything back, but I guess he saw nothing wrong. Maybe it meant nothing to him.

"Mimi?" Liz yelled.

"What?"

"Are you okay? You dazed off."

I did that sometimes.

"Oh, sorry. I'm fine."

"When you say fine, you're not okay, Mimi," Britt said. "We know you."

"Did something happen?" Ash asked.

"No! Of course not." I snapped. They looked confused. "I mean, that was a very traumatizing moment for me. We all almost died. Ms. Jane has a right to be mad." I changed the subject.

"I know. I honestly did not think anything would happen," Britt said to me. "I am so sorry. Not just to Mimi, but to all of you. And what was that lady doing in Ms. Jane's yard anyway?"

"It is okay, Britt, and that is a great question," Ash said. "All that matters is that we are okay and safe."

"We did almost just die," Liz said. "We need to be more careful around here. We can't just pretend like this is a joke. We just found out how serious this was with Team Life and all. We are supposed to be dead, and people are looking for us so they can kill us. That game was stupid."

"That didn't stop you from playing it. You said nothing. At least Ash and Alex said no. You didn't even say anything, so do not blame this on Britt. We are all to blame for this stupid game." I defended Britt. Ash had been irritating me the entire day.

"I'm not saying it is her fault," said Liz. "I am just saying we need to be more careful. That's all." Liz was completely blaming it on Britt. The game was Britt's idea, but we all played. We walked into the game room.

"What happened?" Kendall asked. She looked mad. "You guys are idiots. We could have been killed!" Everything she was saying was sadly true.

"Kendall calm down," Jackson said.

"Calm down? People are trying to kill us!" yelled Kendall. "If you guys were not so calm, then you wouldn't have done something so reckless, so no, I am not going to calm down!"

"Kendall," said Henry.

"I expected more from you and Jackson. Ever since you've been hanging with them three, you have completely lost it. Jackson, you don't get into fights! Henry, you are way too old and mature to be playing a truth or dare game under our circumstances."

"We understand that you're mad, Kendall," Britt said, "but don't you dare blame this on Jackson and Henry. They have the right to choose their friends. Just because you spend the majority of your time chasing after a guy who doesn't want you, doesn't mean they have to do the same. Kendall, no one likes you here. Change your attitude and maybe, you will have friends."

"I don't want your friendship, Britt," Kendall shot back. "This is why all you guys are stupid. We are not here to make friends. We are here to survive. My life may mean nothing to you but think of everyone else's life you put into danger by doing this brainless dare. The kids could have been killed. The very person that is trying to protect us could have been killed. Next time you want to do something so outrageous, think about them." As much as I hated her, she was right.

"We're sorry," I said.

"Ugh. Whatever." And now I am back to hating her. "Where is Alex?" she asked.

"His room. Where else?" Henry said. Kendall walked out of the game room. I was glad she was out of the room. She was making me feel so guilty, and she had a right to.

"I'm sorry," I said to Henry and Jackson.

"It is all of our faults," Henry said.

"Still."

"I am just glad you are alive," Henry said. "What we did was irresponsible, but we have to appreciate the fact that we're all alive and move on."

Henry was right. We were safe and that was all that really mattered at this point.

Chapter 9

The week was finally over, and Ms. Jane began working again. She still glared at us every time we passed her. Having her gone meant that I didn't have to see the disappointment on her face. We tried speaking to the other fugitives, but they were not online. Our guess was that they got caught, but none of us were certain. It was difficult not to think the worse, and after all the hope they gave me, I tried to remain positive. Alex was still in his room as usual, and Kendall, of course, followed. I started to wonder what they did in there, but I didn't think I would want to know. Ever since the incident with Alex, we hadn't talked. I didn't know if he was avoiding me, or if I was avoiding him—maybe it was both.

"So Ms. Jane is still freaking out about the dare thing," said Britt. "As moody as she is, I thought she would get over it by now."

"What we did was messed up guys," I said.

"I know," she said, "but it's Ms. Jane."

"True."

We went downstairs to the kitchen. Strangely, everyone was down there.

"Why are you guys here?" I asked.

"We ran out of food from the other kitchen," Josh said.

"So you're taking from the younger kid's kitchen? Shame on you," Britt said sarcastically and laughed. This was my first time seeing them speak in over a week. It was odd.

"Hey. We all have to eat," he argued with a grin on his face. It confused me even more. The boys continued searching in the pantry for junk food. Even Jason took part in this.

"What are you guys doing?" Alex suddenly appeared. Kendall was right behind him.

"So he lives!" laughed Jackson.

"Haven't seen you in a while," said Henry.

"What are you talking about? We share the same room," Alex said.

"I haven't been in there for a week, Alex. You and Kendall just hog up the place." This was strange. Henry and Alex were friends, and now they weren't talking. "What's up with you?"

"Nothing."

Ding dong. It was the doorbell. We were all silent.

"Who would be ringing the doorbell?" I whispered.

Boom. Boom. They started to knock.

"We have to hide," Henry said. "Liz, Josh, and Jason should go with the kids. Just hide them somewhere. Everyone else hide in the closet." He took charge.

"Hello." It was a male voice. It sounded familiar, but I couldn't point it out.

"He sounds familiar," I said.

"Be quiet," Alex said. He left a crack in the door to see what was going on. The door opened.

"How did that happen? Does he have a key?" Britt asked.

"Shh," Henry said.

"It's David," said Alex.

"Hello! Jane? Is anyone home?" David continued to ask.

Alex started. "I'm kicking his—"

"Don't be stupid, Alex." Henry tried to stop Alex, but he didn't listen. He opened the door and ran towards David. Henry followed. They pushed him down. David was on the floor and appeared to be unconscious.

"What did you guys do?" I asked.

"Get some tape or rope or something," Alex said. They dragged his body into a chair. Kendall found tape and rope and handed it to Alex. Alex and Henry wrapped him in the chair. There was no way he could get out. He was still unconscious.

"Did you kill him?" yelled Britt.

"No, he is just knocked out," Henry said.

"What are we going to do?" I asked.

"What does this even mean?" Ash asked.

"It means that Ms. Jane is not one of the good guys. She is working with the man who tried to kill us! I knew she was evil. None of you guys listened!" Alex yelled.

"There has to be another explanation," I said.

"There isn't one! Ms. Jane doesn't have our best interest at heart! She doesn't care about us!"

"Then why did she save our lives?"

"That is what I'm going to ask him."

"You're being irrational. There has to be a better explanation."

David started to wake up.

"Why are you here? Why are you working with Jane?" Alex demanded an answer. His voice was full of rage.

"Calm down, Son," David said.

Alex punched him in the face. "That is for everything you did to me in the camp." He punched him again. "That is for trying to kill us. Now tell me, what are you doing here?" Alex continued.

"I work with Team Life. I am the one who told Jane to get you," he said. His lip was bloody from Alex punching him.

"Wait. That makes sense," Ash said.

"He's lying!" Alex punched him again.

"That's the truth, Son."

He punched him again.

"Give him a chance to talk Alex," advised Henry.

"Stop!" Kendall yelled. He continued to punch him.

"Alex, stop it!" I yelled on the top of my lungs. David's face was covered in blood and so was Alex's fist. He wiped his hand on his shirt and started to go upstairs.

"Where are you going?" I asked him.

He ignored me. I ran after him and grabbed his arm.

"Leave me alone. You don't want to push me right now."

"You need to stop running away from your problems. All you do is sit in your room doing God knows what with Kendall. It's pathetic. Stop feeling sorry for yourself. All of us are in this position, not just you."

"You don't know me."

"Stop using that as an excuse! We all came from tough backgrounds, and right now, we are all in the same position. If you want to continue acting like a wimp, then go ahead and hide upstairs." I walked downstairs. He didn't move for a while. I walked toward David.

"Someone get him a towel. He needs to be cleaned up." I looked at him. "Now, tell us everything you know," I demanded.

"My name is David Skigh, as you already know. Jane and I go way back. I told her that you guys needed to be protected. She and a few other people created the group Team Life to protect other fugitives. I help her when I can."

"So you are a double agent?" Britt asked.

"I guess you could say that."

"If you and Ms. Jane are so close, then why didn't you know we were here?"

"She told me you guys were safe. She never told me where she was keeping you. If we weren't friends, then I wouldn't have a key to her house." He made a good point.

"Well, she won't be home for a few hours so you are going to have to stay tied up until we know we can trust you," I said. He didn't say anything.

"So is Harold a double agent too? You guys just beat me almost to death for fun?" Alex was still angry.

"He would have killed you. That was the only way he would keep you alive. I'm sorry."

"Are you guys actually falling for this?" Alex said. "He's lying."

"We don't know that," Henry said. "We will figure it out once Ms. Jane is here."

"You trust her? Don't be naive guys."

"We have no reason to think Ms. Jane would want to kill us, Alex. Stop being irrational."

"She had our files!"

"So she could contact our parents to tell them we were safe."

"She had my aunt's file. I didn't even know I had an aunt!"

Everyone got quiet.

"Jane contacted her to tell her you were safe," David said. Alex got even angrier. He walked towards David, but Henry and I got in the way.

"Stop," I said.

"He tried to kill us! How can you guys trust so easily?"

"You shouldn't let your anger get the best of you, Alex," said David. "You guys are in a tough situation, and you need to stick together."

"Shut up!"

"Alex calm down!" He listened to me. I walked over to him. "I understand that you feel betrayed and upset by your aunt. I know it is confusing and scary for you, but we do need you right now. We need you to get through this," I whispered. I saw a tear fall down his face. I had never seen him cry or any of the guys cry for that matter. He always put up a front, but he was scared. I wiped a tear off of his face. "It will be okay. I promise." He hugged me.

"Okay, so you guys are cool now?" Britt asked. "Yay! Anyway, what are we doing with him exactly?"

"Just keep him tied up," Henry said. "Someone has to watch him until Ms. Jane comes back."

"Okay. I guess I will," Britt said. "You probably don't remember me, but I was the one you kidnapped as well."

"How could I forget?"

"Oh good! You do remember. This is exciting," said Britt. "Now, how do you know Ms. Jane?"

"You don't have to answer that," Henry said to David. "Brittney, do not terrorize this person. Wait till Ms. Jane gets here." She did as he said.

"So, do I sit here and watch him not talk?"

"I will sit here with you."

"I will too," suggested Kendall.

Britt looked confused. "I'm sorry, but I thought we didn't like each other."

"David is right, and in a way, so were you. We do need to make friends. In order to survive, we have to stick together." It was the first time she did something without bothering Alex. This was surprising.

"Oh well, okay." Britt smiled.

"I'll go get Liz, Josh, Jason. They need to get the details," Ash said. She walked off.

"I need to talk to you," Alex said to me.

"Okay." I wondered if he was referring to the kiss. I still had no idea what to think about that. He took me to his room. It was not as dirty as I expected. I was surprised to see that there weren't clothes everywhere.

His bed wasn't made, and I saw bags of food on the bed, but that was it. The room was very similar to mine. It was very spacious with two beds. I assume one for him and the other for Henry. Henry's side was much neater than Alex's, but I was surprised by how clean it was. He sat on his bed and moved the bags out of the way. I sat beside him.

I know that I have been weird around you for a while, no kidding. I want to apologize for what I said to you. You have been one of my friends throughout this entire mess, and I'm—I'm sorry for shutting you out."

"It's okay. I understand that you were really upset, and I knew you didn't mean those things, but they hurt so much. Then Kendall was your spokesperson whenever you were gone, and I thought you really didn't trust me. The fact that you confided in her and not me made me second-guessed our trust. I want to be there for you, and I want you to know that you can trust me." It might have been the first time I ever told Alex how I honestly felt.

"I know I can. I felt so angry for hurting you that I couldn't really talk to you, and I have felt so guilty about it and..."

"And?"

"I'm not the type to do this stuff."

"Talk about your feelings?"

"Yeah"

"I noticed. You're the type to shut people out. That's not healthy. You can talk to me and Henry and even Kendall. We all care about you so much." He was quiet. "I'm sorry that you feel otherwise, but we do—I do."

"I know."

"So how are you?"

"What do you mean?"

"About the aunt thing. How are you?" He got quiet. I knew Alex was not one to talk about his feelings at all. He avoided them all the time, but since we were on the topic, I thought he might open up. "We don't have to talk about it."

"My parents died when I was a baby. The only family I had left was her, and she could have raised me. Instead, she put me up for adoption. I just don't understand."

"Usually, parents that adopt someone are not going to treat their child horribly."

"Well, they adopted me because they could not have kids. As time passed, they were able to, and after she was born, it almost felt like they abandoned me. At first, it was fine, but they started to change. They had problems in their relationship, and it took a toll on both me and my sister, but even then, they still weren't awful."

"You have a sister? You've never talked about her. Wait, why is she not here?"

"She died a few years ago from cancer." My heart dropped. I never knew he had been through so much.

"Oh. I'm so sorry, Alex."

"It's fine." He shrugged it off like it wasn't a big deal, but I knew it was. "Guess what her name was."

"What?"

"Meredith." He smiled. "You remind me of her actually. She would get so mad when I messed with her just like you do. I honestly think she rolled her eyes the same way you do. She was optimistic and kind and so innocent. She always had a smile on her face."

"How old was she?"

"She died when she was nine. That is when everything went downhill. My parents didn't know how to handle it. They hated me for being alive when their biological daughter wasn't. My dad even told me that once. My mother- I don't think I have seen her smile since Meredith was still here. It was heartbreaking." I didn't know how to react to this information. I never knew how much Alex had been through or how much he kept inside. I did not know how to help him or if I could even make a difference, so I wrapped my arms around him and held him tightly. That was the only comfort I knew how to create. "I'm so sorry for everything you've been through." Now, I was the one crying.

"Mimi, it's fine. I don't want anyone feeling sorry for me." I wiped my tears.

"I don't feel sorry for you. I just hate everything you had to go through."

"Well, we all have our problems. Now, I just want to understand my aunt. She was all I had left."

"I'm sure your aunt had a good reason. She probably couldn't support you at that time. I don't know, but if you wanted to, maybe once we get out of this mess, you could meet her." "She has never tried to contact me. Why would I do that?"

"Because she is the only person that could tell you about your biological mom and dad, and she's your family." Truth is, I didn't know why his aunt left him. I just didn't want him thinking the worst. Alex harbored so much pain inside that could only be conveyed through anger. Though he tried to joke about everything, there was something missing. I didn't want him to feel that hole. I didn't want him to feel anymore pain, but I couldn't change that. I didn't even know if I had an effect.

It remained silent. I was under the impression that he was done talking about it. He had shared enough for the day, and now, he didn't want to.

"You know that truth or dare game was actually fun." He laughed.

"It was dangerous, Alex. You were the main person against it anyway."

"Yeah, but it was fun. Fooling that lady, pretending we were a couple. She totally bought it."

I thought of the kiss. "Haha. Yeah."

"So," be said. "I'm supposed to have a surprise for you tonight, babe." His smile was back. I didn't get why he was playing a game with me about this.

"That's not funny, Alex."

"I'm just kidding. Calm down."

"You kid too much. I can hardly ever tell when you're serious."

"Why are you getting mad?"

"Because it's frustrating! Everything you do is frustrating. I never know when any of the things you say are sincere"

"You know that's just my personality. I've always been that way and really? After the conversation we just had. I just opened up to you more than I have to anyone."

"Why did you kiss me?" I blurted. I couldn't contain it anymore.

"What?" He wasn't expecting that. I guess he thought I would ignore my problems they way he did, but I wasn't him. He wanted to pretend like nothing happened, but it did.

"You kissed me. Why?"

"We were pretending to be a couple. It was to protect us."

"We had already fooled her. She wasn't even paying us any attention." He got quiet. "So why did you do it?"

"It was to protect us, Mimi. That's all."

"So you don't have any feelings for me?"

"No." He laughed. I shattered. I wondered if he could tell how much his words affected me. Does he know how much I like him? Does he just pretend to be oblivious?

"Okay good! Now, I don't have to let you down easy." I smiled. It was hard not to cry in that moment.

"Because you are such a heartbreaker." He could not be that oblivious.

"Yup."

"Just because you broke Chase's heart does not mean you could break every guy's heart. Don't flatter yourself."

"What about you? You're breaking Kendall's heart."

"Ha. Kendall and I are just friends."

"It's obvious she likes you."

"You know, she said the same thing about you," he said. I didn't know how to respond to that, so I just laughed. I forced it so much. "Oh please. You love me."

"Ha! Okay. Keep thinking that."

"Oh, I know." Seriously, he had to know how I felt about him. "But seriously though, what is going on between you and Kendall?"

"Why? Are you jealous?" His smirk drove me insane but not in a good way. I almost felt disgusted.

"Stop fooling around. I'm serious."

"Not that many people like her. She just sits here and talks to me sometimes. Sometimes, we don't even talk."

I felt like he was implying something else. "What do you do other than talk?"

"Nothing. She doesn't ask any detailed questions about my life, and I like that about her."

"So you do like her."

"I didn't say that."

"You didn't deny it."

"I don't like her. She is just a friend."

I didn't believe him. "I think it's time we go back downstairs." I opened his door. There was Britt.

"Oh! What a coincidence. I was about to go get you." She was lying. She had been standing there the entire time—which meant that she knew Alex and I kissed.

"Yep. What a coincidence." I glared at her. We all walked downstairs. David looked a little better. His face was clean, but you could see the cuts and the bruises.

"Ms. Jane should be here at any moment," Kendall said. We heard the garage minutes later. "She is here." I didn't think we ever really planned out what we were going to do once she got here.

"So, do we just stand here until she comes in?" asked Britt.

"What else would we do?" I asked her back. We heard her opening the door. She was inside. I didn't know why, but I was so nervous. She walked inside and saw us.

"What did you do?" She looked at David and ran towards us.

"I think you owe us an explanation," Henry said.

"Why are you working with the guy who tried to kill us?" Alex's anger was back.

"He saved you guys. He wasn't trying to harm you. He is on our side. I promise."

"Ms. Jane," Britt said, "we know you have been keeping a lot of secrets from us. We aren't stupid."

"What are you talking about?" She sounded so innocent.

"You lied to us about Team Life. We know why you weren't at work last week. Please stop lying to us."

"I am just trying to protect you."

"It makes it a little harder to trust you," I said.

"You have to tell us everything," Ash said.

"First, can you untie David?"

"No. We need to know why he is here first to make sure your stories match up."

"Why are you here?" she asked him.

"I was coming to tell you how the strike went. You never told me you were protecting them at your house."

"Team Life didn't want you to know. You are working for both sides, and the safety of the children is the most important thing."

"So you lied."

"I didn't lie. I told you they were safe."

"But you didn't trust me?"

"Do not make this about you and me right now. Of course I trust you, but other people don't, and it wouldn't hurt if you didn't know their whereabouts." It seemed like there was something else going on between Ms. Jane and David. "Will you guys untie him now!" She was angry. We did as she asked. "How long did they have you like this?"

"A few hours."

"I'm sorry. What happened to your face?" David looked at Alex.

"I fell," he said. Ms. Jane new something was up, but she ignored it.

"So what do you know?"

"The strike did hurt the economy but not as much as we thought it would. It wasn't bad enough for them to consider withdrawing the act."

"So it was unsuccessful?" she said. "Great."

"We still have more time. Citizens are outraged. It will get better."

"What do we do now?"

"There is a protest next month. Team Life followers are planning it. I am not sure if it would be wise for you guys to show up since you are someone of a higher status. It will be suspicious. However, there are thousands of people that will be marching in the downtown area, so that can also help."

"I will make sure everyone knows." She smiled.

"It's getting late. I think I should go," David said.

"You can stay for dinner!" I knew what Britt was thinking. She thought sparks would fly tonight. "You can if you want to. I'm making lasagna," Ms. Jane said.

"All right, I will." He smiled.

"Well," said Britt, "we will be going upstairs now." She ran upstairs and everyone followed.

"See, Alex," said Kendall. "He is not a killer."

"Whatever."

Kendall laughed. I was for sure something was going on between them. There was no way you can spend that much time with each other, alone, in a room, and not do anything.

"They are such a cute couple." Britt squirmed.

"Britt," said Ash. "They are fully capable of getting together if they want to. Do not mess anything up."

"I am not doing anything!" she lied.

"We have more important things to discuss," I said. "Like the strike."

"What are we going to do about that?" asked Ash.

"We are going to go." Everyone looked at me like I was crazy.

"You're insane," Kendall said.

"No way," Jackson said.

"You're not going!" Alex yelled.

"We need to do something about this," I said, "I am tired of sitting here and not defending ourselves"

"We will get in so much trouble if we do this," Britt said.

"We're not doing it. Remember the prank. I thought we learned our lesson." Alex was mad.

"This isn't a prank. This is our life," I argued.

"This is a little daring," Henry admitted, "but I understand why you want to do it."

"We need to."

"We need to stay safe," Alex said.

"Agreed. You are an even bigger idiot than I thought if you want to do this!" Kendall yelled.

"Hey! What happened to sticking together?" Brit said.

"Sorry. Bad habit. Look, we will be risking our lives if we go out there."

"This is something to consider," Ash said.

"No, it's not. Mimi," said Alex, "you are not going out there." He was still being protective. It was because I remind him of his little sister. It made sense now, but why would he kiss me? I still didn't understand.

"We can talk about this later," I suggested, "but everyone at least think about it."

"Ok…No."

"Alex. Stop trying to protect her," Kendall said. "She can make her own decisions and if none of us agrees, there is no way she can go alone anyway." That was true.

"Just consider it," I said. I walked to my room to be alone and lay on the bed. It was a long day.

"Mimi, we need to talk!" It was Britt and Ash. I guess there was no way I was getting any peace and quiet in this house.

"What?"

"You know what!" She was referring to the kiss.

"I don't really trust sitting here in this room just so people can listen by the door. It is frustrating."

"Whisper," Britt whispered.

"You were standing right there Britt. You already know what happened."

"Yeah, but how! When did this happen?"

"We pretended to be a couple, and somewhere along the way, he kissed me," I whispered.

"So he likes you?"

"Britt you were listening to our conversation. He said no!"

"He was lying."

"No, he wasn't."

"Then why would he kiss you? You said so yourself that the lady wasn't even looking at you." Good point, but I didn't want to think about it.

"I don't care. Let's not talk about it." I did care; I did want to talk about it but with him.

"Okay fine, whatever."

"Your idea is crazy by the way," Ash said.

"I kind of wish I thought of it," Britt said.

"We should seriously do it though. I mean why not?" I asked.

"Well, if we get caught, Ms. Jane would get mad at us, we could die, Ms. Jane could die—shall I go on?" Ash said.

"Ash has a point," agreed Britt. I was surprised she wasn't on my side.

"I don't know how many people will be up for this, Mimi," Ash said.

"I can go by myself."

"Because you can drive, right?" Britt said.

"We all know there is no way Alex will let her go by herself."

"He likes her." Britt emphasized on "like." She and Ash were laughing.

"Shut up!" I threw a pillow at Britt's faced.

"Just admit it. He does."

"He denied liking me, and didn't I say I don't want to talk about it?"

"Why? Haven't you been like waiting for this moment since you met him?" asked Britt.

"I think something is going on with Kendall," I whispered.

"Kendall?" They said at the same time.

"Shh!"

"Why would you think that?" Ash asked.

"They're together all the time in his room. Britt, you heard him say 'and sometimes, we don't talk.' What do you think that meant?"

"That he tells her to shut up and be quiet, or she has to leave. Since no one really likes her, she has nowhere else to go." laughed Britt.

"I'm serious, but let's forget about that too! What is up with you and Henry?" I asked. I was so curious.

"And Josh?" Ash added.

"Are you and Josh together?" I asked.

"No. We broke up a long time ago."

"What! You didn't tell us," I yelled.

"Why?" Ash asked.

"Well, it wasn't really a big deal. We are just better off being friends. We still are friends."

"Something had to have happened."

Britt seemed nervous to tell us. "I was not what he was looking for in a relationship. Umm...we had different interest."

I was confused. He didn't like her anymore. "What does that mean?"

"Look, it is something really personal for him. I can't go around telling people. That would ruin his life," she said. I kind of had a feeling where this was going.

"Well, what about you and Henry?"

She laughed at the question. "Henry and I are just friends."

"Really?" I said, "I don't think so."

"I am dead serious. Our relationship isn't like you and Alex. I actually do feel like he is my older brother." That was such a lie. Someone knocked on the door.

"Food is ready." It sounded like Kendall. We walked to the kitchen. Everyone was at the kitchen downstairs. Not all of us could sit around the table, so I didn't understand how that was going to work. I saw David and Ms. Jane. They were laughing and having a good time. Maybe Britt's cupid skills were working.

"This smells amazing, Ms. Jane. You have no idea how much I love lasagna." It was true. I loved lasagna more than almost anything. "Thank you, Mimi." She made cheese garlic toast—the best bread to have with lasagna. I was definitely going to feast tonight.

"So David..." I had to ask. "You were talking about a strike next month."

"Yes. Team Life followers are planning on having one downtown."

"Really, that is so bold. When?" I wasn't fooling anyone.

"Mimi, you're not going," Ms. Jane said.

"I'm not interested. I was just curious." I knew I shouldn't lie to Ms. Jane, but I also knew that no one felt like it was important for us to go.

"Mimi, you are a terrible liar," Alex said. That was also true, but I was able to trick him to thinking I didn't like him. I must not be that bad.

"I'm sorry, Mimi," David said. "I know you want to make a difference, but it is best that you guys stay in the house. You are safe and protected here. We cannot risk it." It was better for us to just stay here, but I needed to protest. No one will recognize us.

"So, you aren't going to tell me the date?"

"Mimi, do you want to get killed? Because sometimes, it sounds like you do?" Alex said. "You are not going."

"She was just asking a question, Alex. Calm down," Britt defended me.

"I wasn't kidding when I said you guys need to be unified. That is the only way you will get through this. Stop bickering about small things. You need to be on the same page." David was right. He seemed to be right about everything.

"Mimi, I say this because I care about you. Stop asking questions about it. We are not going." Alex was serious, and I was tired of him telling me what to do. Other people wanted to do this just as much as I did. They just didn't know it yet.

Chapter 10

"I'm leaving now. Don't try and get us killed!" Ms. Jane yelled. She was going to work. She finally trusted us—she knew it would be better than not telling us anything. If she didn't tell us anything, we were going to sneak to find information, and after everything that had happened, she didn't want that. She closed the door and walked into the garage. Soon, I heard the garage door go up, and she was gone.

Everyone was in the kitchen eating breakfast. Andrew and John were eating with us as well. Even the younger girls, Perry and Taylor, were in the kitchen eating with us. They were usually in the playroom by themselves.

"It's been over a week," Britt said. Every day, we would try to contact the other team at noon, but they would never answer—either their Team Life member caught them, or the government caught them.

"I know. It's starting to scare me." I was hoping that it was just their leader. Anything else was too scary to think of.

"Should we ask Ms. Jane?" questioned Josh.

"That would be stupid Josh," Chase said. Everyone was treating him normally now. After seeing David, we all tried to stay close—it was important.

"I don't know," said Ash, "If we still don't hear from them today, then maybe, it wouldn't be such a bad idea." I agreed with her. We were worried, and if we didn't know the truth, then we were never going to find out.

"Their leader's name was Mr. Haun, right?" Alex asked.

"I think so," Ash said.

"I still don't know if that is a good job," Chase said. "She just started trusting us, and if we tell her, there's a chance she won't trust us again."

"She knows we knew about Team Life before David told us," Kendall said.

"Or maybe, she just assumed we knew because David told us." I was certain she assumed. There was no way she could have known that we knew for over a week before she told us.

"If they don't answer today," Henry said, "then we can worry about asking Ms. Jane or not. Let's just hope and pray they do." That was all we could do: hope and pray.

We were still in the kitchen. Everyone was done eating, and no one was talking. We sat in silence for a long time. I looked at everyone: Henry was standing next to Brittney, then Kendall next to Jackson, Jackson next to Ashley, Ashley was next to me, and I was sitting down at the table, Alex sat across me, and Josh and Chase were beside him.

If something had happened to the other team, it made this so much more real than we were thinking. We had been safe—Ms. Jane kept us from the news, from everything, so it seemed unreal to us, or at least to me. We had never known someone that had died because of this. We might know someone now. All I could think about was Layla. Her positive liveliness affected me. She was so energetic and social, and then her reserved twin sister was so quiet. I was truly scared for them. All of us were. They were the first people we knew who were in the same position. If they die, where would that leave us?

"So, how has everyone's day been?" Britt tried to break the awkward silence.

"It's been great! There are so many toys to play with here!" Perry said with excitement. I always wondered how Ms. Jane had so many toys. From being in her home, it seemed that she would have wanted to have children. Ignoring the decorative glass, she had toys and rooms specifically designed for children. Yet, Ms. Jane never wanted children. "It's been pretty boring," Andrew said. "Do you guys have any more news for us?"

"What do you mean?" I asked.

"You know what he means," John said. I didn't want to tell them there was a possibility that the other team of fugitives were dead. They did not need to hear something so…gruesome.

"Well, we haven't been able to get in touch with the other team members, but we are still trying. Other than that, we really don't know when we are going to be able to leave." We didn't know that much. Everything I told them was everything I knew—which was nothing.

"So you guys don't know anything?"

"There are still people out there trying to save us."

"But you don't know if it's actually working."

"We don't know how successful they have been, but I am sure more and more citizens are becoming aware of everything that is going on right now."

"That doesn't mean they're supporting us. Are we ever getting out of here?"

"Yes, we are." I couldn't predict the future. I honestly had no clue what was going to happen.

"But you don't know that. No one does." He was irritated.

"Look," Alex said, "we don't know what's going to happen in the next hour. All we can do is hope. Just eat your breakfast for now." The boy accepted it and continued eating. The rest of breakfast was quiet.

I finished my food and went upstairs. No one followed. I went into my room and lied on the bed. I instantly started to cry. I didn't know what went over me. It was like I had been subconsciously fighting these tears for months and now, alone, I could finally let them out. I cried about everything: my mom, my friends, the other fugitives, being confined in this house, Alex, and overwhelming fear of death. It was the first time I ever truly feared dying since we were taken. Death was something we all would mock. It seemed surreal to me—even on the trails. We all thought we were going to die, but it never sunk in, at least not for me. Now, it was. I didn't want to die at fourteen going on fifteen. I was barely a teenager. I didn't even know what career I wanted, or what path I wanted to take in life. Maybe now, I didn't have to worry about those things anyway, but I wanted to worry. I wanted to live. I wanted my friends to live. I wanted my life to be normal again. I wanted to have all these desires. I deserved them. I deserved a normal life. Regardless, my life will never be normal again. Even if I did survive, I could never forget this experience. I had seen too much, and my life would never be the same. None of ours will. If we die, what happens then? Will some other fugitives live and be recognized as the "children who survived?" Will everyone that died just represent a number in a history book—10,000 murdered? That was what will be remembered. Not a name, not a face, not a single memory, but a number. I didn't want to die like this. I didn't want my friends—the thought of my friends gone was frightening. Ash's generosity, Britt's stubbornness, and Liz's honesty would all be gone. I couldn't bear the thought of them being gone. I closed my eyes, but tears still fell all over my face. My heart ached so much. I was curled up in a ball on my bed with no idea if I could ever move out of that position. I heard someone come in the room. I didn't move. I remained curled up. The door closed. I didn't know if they were still in the room because the only thing I could hear were my sobs. Someone lied beside me on the bed and wrapped their arms around me.

"Everything will be okay," Alex said. His words were comforting but not convincing.

"We're going to die." It was inevitable in my mind.

"I won't let that happen." He kissed me on the forehead, and then draped both of his arms around me almost as a shield. I felt safe.

I woke up. He was still beside me with his arms as my shield. I turned to face him. His eyes were open, at first, they were staring in a distance, but then, he was focused on me.

"How long was I out?"

"Not long."

"What time is it?"

"Around two."

I jerked up.

"Did everyone talk to the other fugitives? Are they okay? What happened?" I asked in a matter of two seconds.

"Calm down. Don't worry about it." There was something he wasn't telling me.

"Alex," He noticed my austere tone, but didn't proceed to tell me anything.

"You need to rest." He stroked my arm.

"Tell me what happened," I demanded.

"No." He was so stern. It was hard winning against him. We were both so stubborn.

"Fine, I will find out myself!" I got up, but he pulled me back. "Let go!" He did as I said. I got up and walked to the door. He grabbed me again and carried me to the bed. I screamed and kicked. "Let go! Let go!" He put me back on the bed then sat in a chair beside me.

"Calm down."

"They're dead aren't they?" He didn't respond. "Aren't they!"

"We don't know. We still need to talk to Ms. Jane about it." They were gone. It was a given, and now, we were going to be too. Alex could tell what I was thinking. "If they are gone, it gives us a better reason to keep fighting. We're not going to have the same fate as them." I was really trying to believe this, but it wasn't working. Layla was gone. My faith was gone. "We are going to end up just like them."

"We don't know what state they're in."

"Yes, we do." He was silent. He didn't want to admit it, but he knew. Everyone knew. They got caught. They were dead. We were next, end of discussion. Alex looked at me with desperation. He wanted to find the right words, but there were not any that could change my mind.

"I won't let anything happen to you." There was something genuine about that statement. He really believed it, and for a second, maybe longer, I did too.

"How do I remind you of her?" He knew whom I was talking about.

"I already told you, but you guys are very different."

"How?"

"Just the way you guys react to things. It could be because of age or the situation we are in, but you guys are very different. For instance, everything that was on her mind, she would say out loud. She would never hold back."

"You think I hold back?"

"Not necessarily. You're just different. I don't know how to explain it." He was right, I did hold back though.

I didn't tell him everything I felt, but neither did he. "I think you need to rest more."

"I've been resting all day. I'm fine."

"Are you?"

"Yes." I really didn't know. I wasn't crying anymore. I thought I was fine.

"I don't believe you."

"I'm trying really hard to accept it."

"Accept what?"

"Our fate."

"You shouldn't be so willing to give up."

"I'm being pragmatic."

"You're giving up."

There was nothing to stay on. Our fate was decided months ago, and there was nothing we could do about it. "We are already dead."

"No, we're not! There is so much we can still do. Staying alive is one of them." It was a never-ending argument. The sooner Alex realized that, the better.

"I don't know what's gotten into you, Mimi. You are usually the strongest."

"I'm tired of being so positive. We all are, but the truth is we have a better chance at learning how to fly than getting out of this alive!" I yelled. His eyebrow rose as if he had finally realized something.

"We're all scared, Mimi. It's not an excuse to give up."

"I'm not giving up! Please stop saying that," I told him, and it was quiet for a while.

"Please rest."

"I'm well rested. You are keeping me in this room like a prisoner."

"You can leave if you want." I didn't feel like it. I would leave to do what? Go talk to Ashley and Brittney? They probably wondered why Alex has been in my room all day. I did not want to go back and have to deal with that right now. I would much rather stay in here until Ms. Jane came back. I gave Alex an evil looked and tried to "rest" as Alex suggested. I knew he was smirking behind me. He always knew I wouldn't leave the room.

I wasn't tired anymore. I had just fallen asleep in the middle of the day with Alex. Had Alex been with me this entire time? Why did he come into my room in the first place? He must have needed something because Alex was hardly ever in my room unless he needed to talk to me about something urgent.

"Hey, Alex."

"Yes?"

"Why did you come into my room earlier? Did you need something?"

"I just came to check up on you. You were in here for a long time."

I laughed at that. "Ha. When do you ever just check up on me?"

"When I'm worried," he said. Why was he worried? I guess finding me in my room having a nervous break-down did not help his nerves.

"I'm fine, Alex. You don't need to worry about me."

"That is another thing that is different about you and my sister. Meredith never was afraid to admit she needed help. You never want people to know when you're hurt, at least that's how I see you." I was slightly offended by this statement. It took months before I even knew he had a sister. He never asks people for help or advice, not even for someone to just listen. I turned around to face him.

"And you do?" I said defensively. Lucky for him someone knocked on the door then proceeded to open it. I asked myself. *What was the point of knocking if you were just going to open it before a response?*

"Ms. Jane is home and has ordered pizza. It is in the downstairs kitchen," Henry said. "Hope I didn't disturb anything." Alex was sitting in a chair beside my bed while I was in it. I didn't know what assumptions he made.

"You didn't. Thanks, Henry," I said. I got out of bed. I was a little dizzy since I hadn't eaten since breakfast, and it was already dinner.

"Are you okay?"

"Yes, just hungry." We walked downstairs to the kitchen table. Everyone was already in a chair, so I had to pull up a chair to eat.

The pizza slices were huge. I had never seen such a large pizza in my life. I swore it was heaven in my mouth. It could have been my starvation, but others seemed to react the same.

"This pizza is great, Ms. Jane," Britt said. "I've never tasted anything like it."

"I can't take the credit. David made it for you guys." At that instant, I believe every guy said "Ohhh." "Oh, hush kids," she said while trying not to blush.

"Someone likes David. Someone likes David," Chase said. Josh laughed. I never realized how immature some of the guys were. Ms. Jane continued to pretend like she didn't hear us.

"Tell him we all say thank you," I told her.

"I will make sure to," assured Ms. Jane. We all continued to enjoy the pizza, but I knew what was coming. Someone was eventually going to ask about the other fugitives.

"There's something we need to tell you, Ms. Jane," Britt started. She waited until Ms. Jane was done with her food. She was already suspicious.

"Go on."

"Well," started Britt, "a long time ago, we snuck into your office to gain more information on Team Life. We found files of us and a way to contact other Team Life member—" Ms. Jane interrupted Britt.

"You did what! I just started to trust you guys, and this is what you have been doing behind my back."

"Ms. Jane, you have to understand that you weren't telling us anything," Henry said. "We wanted information."

"There's more to the story," continued Britt. "We found other fugitives that a Team Life member was housing. They told us about the strike and everything. They were supervised by a man named Dr. Haun." Ms. Jane's anger instantly turned into concern.

"We haven't been able to contact them since the strike. Do you know if anything has happened to them?" Alex asked.

And it was written all over her face. They were dead, just as we suspected.

"They're dead," I blurted out. Ms. Jane was shocked by what I said and how blunt I said it.

"Don't be so morbid, Mimi," Liz argued.

"But they are, aren't they?" I asked. Ms. Jane continued to talk.

"We have not been able to reach Dr. Haun either," she said. "Our best assumption is that they were caught and killed. It is possible that Dr. Haun and his fugitives escaped, but we have no knowledge of what has happened," she said. She got up and put her dish in the sink. "You can do the dishes tonight." I saw a tear fall down her chin. I felt bad for how crude I was with her feelings. She probably knew Dr. Haun really well, and there being a possibility he was gone, probably hurt her more than anything. She left the kitchen.

"So what does this mean?" Kendall asked. Everyone already knew the answer though. It was predictable.

"It means we're dead." No one responded.

Chapter 11

I pretty much stayed in my room for the last couple of weeks. It wasn't like there was anything to do. People continued to have faith and set up meetings to get out of this mess, but I didn't go. There was no faith left in me. I was slowly, but surely, accepting death. I kept picturing Layla's smile. I remembered the way her eyes lightened when she first saw us. Her body was filled with excitement. I remembered the optimism she gave me, but I knew the light had left her eyes, along with the hope they brought. Ash, Britt, and Liz would always try and convince me, but nothing could change my mind. Alex would try too, but after a while, he stopped and would just sit in complete silence. There wasn't much to say unless you were trying to construct a plan to keep us from being fugitives. It was irrelevant. All of these meetings were unnecessary—we were not going to make it out alive. I would never see my mother again—end of discussion.

Boom. Boom. Someone was knocking on the door. I didn't respond. They came in anyway.

"I didn't say come in." I turned around. It was Jackson.

"Hey." He ignored my impoliteness and sat on the windowsill.

"Did Ashley send you in here?"

"Actually, Alex did." That was surprising.

"And exactly, why did he think you would change my mind?"

"I can be pretty persuasive." He grinned.

"I can be pretty stubborn." He started looking out at the window. Nothing was said for a few minutes. He opened the window. No one had ever opened the window. We would be at risk of a neighbor seeing us.

"What are you doing?"

"I'm getting fresh air."

I ran up and shut it! "Are you crazy! You could get everyone caught."

"So you do still care? This will be a little easier than I thought." He smiled.

"I don't know what you're talking about. Just please leave my room." I tried to be as polite as possible. His eyes were focused on the window. "Get out!" I yelled. He still didn't acknowledge my presence. "Jackson!"

"Isn't that the lady that caught you and Alex out-side?" He pointed to the house across from ours. I looked out. It was Mrs. Wilson. It looked like she was saying something to a man who was probably her hus-band—except his clothes weren't as posh as I expected. He was wearing a T-shirt and jeans. He appeared to be much younger than Mrs. Wilson. He seemed to be no older than twenty-five. They were mumbling some-thing and laughing, and then she kissed him.

"What is she doing?"

"I don't know," he said, "but it's definitely not her husband." She continued to kiss him passionately. She took the man's shirt off. Then I heard a large flash. Jackson was taking a picture.

"Why are you taking pictures?

"Insurance."

I knew what he meant. If Mrs. Wilson ever found out who we were, a picture will keep her from telling the police. "You think she's a threat?" Mrs. Wilson clothes the curtains. We couldn't see anything anymore.

"Better safe than sorry. She's been spying on this house. I've seen her. She suspects something."

I guess Alex and I weren't as convincing as we believed.

"Do you see that?"

I looked into Mrs. Wilson's driveway. A car was parked in front of the house. A man in a grey suit got out of the car. He seemed to be Mrs. Wilson's age.

"I guess Mr. Wilson's home," laughed Jackson.

"This is like watching reality TV."

Mr. Wilson unlocked the door and went into the house.

"Now, we can't see anything." Jackson was as intrigued as I was.

Then the curtains were opened. The young man was rushing to find a place to hide. He went under the bed. Mrs. Wilson left the room.

"Really? The bed. There is no way he's not getting caught." This really felt like reality television.

"We'll see. I'm guessing she left the room so her husband doesn't go in there, so maybe he won't." Jackson thought she wouldn't get caught. Mr. Wilson walked into the room.

"Sweetie, have you been sleeping around?" Jackson said in a low pitch voice. I laughed.

"Of course not, Love, you're the only one for me." Mrs. Wilson was trying to calm her husband.

"Because you know what happens if I catch you cheating. Don't forget we signed a prenup. You will be back on the streets," Jackson said.

"Oh baby, don't be so paranoid. You know I love you." Mrs. Wilson kissed him on the lips.

"Well, I have to get back to work now. Cook me some pot roast tonight."

"Of course, lovehunny." He left the room. Jackson and I looked at each other and started laughing. It might have been the first time I had laughed in weeks. The younger man got under the bed. He left the house as well.

"Well, that was interesting," I said.

"Who knew there would be so much drama in the suburbs?" We laughed. I turned to look out the window. Mrs. Wilson was staring at us.

"Duck!" We both were lying on our stomach. After ten seconds, I looked back up, and her curtains were closed. "She is on her way here," I told him.

"What do we do? We can't just open the door."

"That's exactly what we do."

"That's the dumbest idea ever! Are you insane?"

"She already met Alex and me. We just have to open the door for her."

"I don't know, Mimi."

I ran out of my room to get Alex. He was in the kitchen.

"Alex! Long story short, Mrs. Wilson caught us spying on her, and now she's on her way over here. She knows you and me, so we both can distract her."

"What! I swear, Mimi…" He was angry. He looked at Jackson. "You were supposed to be helping her, not getting all of us killed!"

"Mrs. Wilson is on her way, everyone hide!" Without question everyone hid. Jackson got the children and hid them upstairs. Ash and Britt seemed confused but followed Jackson along with everyone else.

"It's like you have a death wish," Alex said.

"Can you not be a jerk right now?"

"And then you expect me to be there every single time. First, when you guys played truth or dare, and now, this?"

I was appalled. "No one told you to follow me Alex. You didn't have to go out there if you didn't want to, and do not sit here and pretend like you haven't made any reckless decisions either. Goodness, I'm not perfect." The doorbell rang. "Please, pretend like you love me for this."

"You too."

"I don't have to." It kind of just came out. I wasn't sure if it was a thought, or if I said it out loud. I was too scared to look at Alex's face for clarification. Mrs. Wilson started banging on the door. Alex opened it.

"Hey, Mrs. Wilson," Alex said.

"Where is Ms. Jane?"

"She isn't here at this very moment. Is everything okay?"

"Everything is fine. I want to speak with Ms. Jane."

"She isn't here. She'll be home in maybe an hour or two. I will make sure to tell her you stopped by."

"I'll wait till she gets back." She walked inside the house. She looked at me. I thought she came here to yell, but she wasn't. She just smiled at me.

"Would you like something to drink?"

"Yes, some sweet tea please." She walked in and sat at the kitchen table. "I'm sorry, but I don't remember your names."

"My name is Mathew, and this is my girlfriend, Stacy." Of all names, he had chosen Stacy. I smiled.

"Well, Stacy come sit by me! I want to know more about you." She grinned. Something about her smile seemed artificial. I didn't like it. I sat across from her.

"I hope it is sweet enough." Alex handed her the tea and sat beside me.

"This is delicious, thank you."

"So how has your day been?" I asked her. I already knew the answer to that question.

"Wonderful, and yours?"

"Pretty boring, actually. I have been in my room all day." I smiled. I decided to play along with her game. She didn't seem to enjoy it.

"Oh, hunny, am I boring you?" Alex said.

"Of course not, you are perfect." I smiled.

"So tell me, how did you guys meet?"

"On a hiking trip," Alex said. "She kept staring at me, so we finally decided to talk to one another."

"So not true! You were staring at me." I couldn't belief he remembered that.

"Because you kept staring at me!" He looked at Mrs. Wilson. "She would stare at me, and once I looked her way, she would instantly turn back around. I remember laughing so hard." He started to laugh.

"You're so mean!" I rolled my eyes. I knew I was supposed to be affectionate, but I couldn't believe he was telling her the truth.

"I thought it was cute." He held my hand. I couldn't tell if that was true or not. "Anyway, after that, we spoke with each other frequently, and at first, I saw her as a friend, but then I realized she was so much more than that." In my head, I said, *Is this a joke?*

"That is so cute! What happened after that?" Mrs. Wilson asked. She actually seemed intrigued.

"Honestly, I hid my feelings for her for months. I don't know why, but I was scared. Then one day, I kissed her. I don't know what came over me, but I just did. Later, she asked me about the kiss, and I told her it meant nothing. It was just in the heat of the moment, but I knew it did."

"Why did you tell me it didn't mean anything?" I asked him, "You have no idea how much that hurt."

"It just wasn't a good time for us. Telling you how I felt would've made it that much harder to lose you. I couldn't lose you."

"Instead, you chose to push me away."

"It wasn't like that, Stacy."

"That's exactly how it was."

"Listen to me." He looked into my eyes and held both of my hands. "If I told you, it would have been so hard to let you go. I couldn't lose you. I can't lose you." I didn't know if this was real. I didn't know if he was serious or not, and why he chose to tell me in this way. He never made sense to me.

"Why would you have lost her?" asked Mrs. Wilson.

"She was supposed to move to England," he told her. She believed it.

"Back to the story, I finally decided to tell her how I felt and how much I cared for her, and now, we are here." He smiled.

"That is adorable. You must really love her?" Mrs. Wilson said.

"More than she will ever know." He kissed my forehead. I was stunned. I couldn't move or even smile. I just didn't understand.

"I'm sorry. I have to go to the bathroom." I ran upstairs. Right as I reached the top of the stairs, I saw Ashley, Brittney, and Liz standing right in front of me. "What are you guys doing?" I whispered.

"We were listening. Did Alex just say he loved you? I knew it!"

"I can't tell if he is kidding or not. You guys should be hiding!" I walked to my room.

"It's not like she's going to come upstairs," Britt said.

"Just stay in my room." I walked out of my room and went back downstairs.

"That was quick," Mrs. Wilson said. I sat back down.

"So what exactly brings you here, Mrs. Wilson?" I asked. I knew the only reason why she was here: because she knew I saw her cheating on her husband, but so far, she hadn't brought it up.

"When I met y'all, I wasn't the nicest person. I wanted to apologize for my actions." I knew what she wanted now; she didn't want me to tell Ms. Jane about the affair. That honestly wasn't even on my mind. The only way I would ever use that information was if she found out the truth about us. She was too preoccupied with her affair, so I doubt she would ever become a threat.

"It's okay, Mrs. Wilson," I told her, "You just thought we were fugitives. Don't worry, we didn't tell Ms. Jane that you were rude to us, and we have no intentions on telling her." She got the message and calmed down.

"Oh, well thank you. I'm glad the misunderstanding is cleared up. I'm truly sorry for thinking you were fugitives. I was a minute away from turning you guys in."

"That would have been awful," Alex said.

"Yes, it would have. It's a good move the government is making though. The world is getting too over-populated, and let's be honest here, those children would end up somewhere doing drugs and committing crimes. It definitely lowers the crime rate too. After this is over, I will feel even safer in my home." It was taking all of my strength to not slap her across from the table.

"Yeah, definitely. I never thought about it that way. You're so right."

I looked over at Alex. He was clutching his fist.

"Is everything all right, Mathew?" Mrs. Wilson was noticing how tense Alex had gotten. "Yes, I am fine." I touched his forehead.

"I think you're getting a fever! You seem pretty hot."

"It is possible," Alex said.

"Anyway, those stupid liberals who are actually protesting against the law are planning some kind of march downtown. It's rumored at least."

I had completely forgotten about the march. "That's interesting. Do you know when?"

"Why do you want to know, Stacy?" Alex knew what I was thinking. "You're not interested, are you?"

"No! I am just curious."

"It is supposed to happen next Tuesday at noon, but who knows. I won't be going to that stupid thing. I'm sure cops will be all over the place."

All of a sudden, I heard the garage. Ms. Jane was home. She opened the door. She walked into the kitchen and saw Mrs. Wilson.

"Hey, Jane!"

"Hey, what are you doing here?"

"I was just checking on the kids. You shouldn't leave them here for too long alone." Ms. Jane forced a laugh.

"I trust them!" That was a lie. "Would you like to stay for dinner? We're having pork chops."

"No, thank you. You know I am a vegetarian, Jane. It was nice seeing you though."

"Let me walk you out." Ms. Jane walked Mrs. Wilson to the door. They discussed for a few minutes before she was gone.

"Why was she here?" Ms. Jane asked us.

"She rang the doorbell. Since she knew Alex and me, we just decided to let her in."

"Why?"

"We thought she would get suspicious if we didn't. She saw me from my window in my room, so she knew I was here." I decided to leave out the details of Jackson and me spying on her. "According to Jackson, she's been spying on the house, Ms. Jane. I believe I cleared her from her suspicions."

"Well, we need to keep our guard up," she said, "and don't ever open the door for a stranger again." Ms. Jane wasn't her normal, moody, bubbly self. She should have been screaming at us, but instead, she was very distant. She must had felt betrayed by us when we told her that we went through her office, or maybe, she was still coping with the thought of Dr. Haun's death. Maybe she lost faith too. "Dinner will be ready in about two hours. Go upstairs." I started to walk up stairs. "Alex, stay. I need to talk to you."

"Okay," said Alex.

Why did she need to talk to Alex? She never spoke with any of us alone. I went upstairs to my room. Everyone was hiding in my room. "What happened?"

"Nothing really," I said to them, "but we need to have a meeting after dinner. I will tell you guys everything."

"Can we go?" Taylor asked me. I forgot about the children. John and Andrew were a pain in the butt, so there was no forgetting them, but I always forgot about the little girls. I didn't think I had spoken with Taylor or Perry since our first week here.

"You guys will have to go to bed," Ash said.

"That's not fair! Y'all always do this to us!" said John angrily.

"We aren't five years old! Most of us are ten or older. I believe we deserve to know," Andrew backed him up. They just felt the same way we had felt about Ms. Jane. Eventually, they would just go behind our backs to receive more information, so we might as well tell them.

"They have a point. I think we should just tell them," I offered.

"I agree," responded Henry and Jackson.

"Okay," I said, "so the lady that Alex and I have been stalling for the past hour was a little suspicious of us. She believed we were fugitives, which we are, but if she found that out, we would more than likely die. Anyway, I think Alex and I cleared that up, so she shouldn't be spying on us as Jackson said she was, but that is not the big news." I didn't know if it was a smart idea to tell everyone. I wasn't for sure if they would back me up.

"Go on, Mimi," Chase said.

"She told me the date of the march."

"Mimi, we aren't doing it!" Kendall yelled. "What is wrong with you?"

"I think we should. Not all of us, maybe just four or five, but I think it is important we go! I'm tired of just sitting here and not doing anything. We have been waiting to hear if this will law will be deemed unconstitutional. It has been months, and we haven't heard anything. Well now, we have an opportunity to do something about it."

"I knew I could get you out of your jazz," Jackson said. "I'm totally in Mimi." Ash looked at him. "No, you're not!" she said angrily. She acted like Alex.

"I'll be fine, Ash. Don't worry."

"We will be disguised," I said. "That way people won't recognize us."

"No, Mimi." Alex walked in. "I'm completely against it."

"I'm in," Henry said.

"I'm in," Britt said.

"You're not going, Mimi," Alex said.

"I already have people that are willing to go, Alex," I told him. "You're not going to stop me." He knew I was right. I had three people backing me up now. He couldn't stop me.

"Fine. I'll go, but only to protect you. I know how careless you can be."

"Okay," I said. "Well, five is plenty. The rest of you are going to stay here and take care of them." I pointed at Taylor and Perry.

"Does this mean we will see our families soon?" Perry asked me.

"Maybe. It depends on how all of this works out. Now, it's time for all of you to go to sleep." All of them walked out without a fight. I was surprised that John and Andrew didn't say anything. They just walked out of the room.

"So exactly, how are we going to leave without Ms. Jane noticing?" Britt asked.

"She has more than one car," I said. "I'm sure we can find the keys somewhere. We will have to be back before six though. Otherwise, we will get caught."

"I know how to hot-wire a car," Henry said. He noticed how appalled all of us were. "I haven't ever stolen a car or anything like that. I'm into engineering and mechanics. You guys know this."

"Okay, okay, we believe you," Britt said. "People know how we look. How effective are our disguises really going to be?" She had a point. It's not like we could just put on sunglasses, and no one will know who we are.

"We might have to do something drastic than like cutting our hair or dying it," I suggested. Britt was completely uninterested.

"Or we could just wear hoodies and sunglasses," Henry said.

"Seriously! We are going to be around people that support us anyway," Britt said.

"People that don't might be there too. You have no idea." Alex made a valid point.

"I'm not cutting my hair," said Britt.

"Fine. Sweatshirts and sunglasses it is." Henry stayed firm to his suggestion.

"Do we even know how to get there?" Jackson asked.

"We will find out on the internet tomorrow," I answered.

"Okay, this sounds like a plan." Britt was excited.

"I still think this is a stupid idea," Kendall hissed. She seemed irritated. I thought many people were: Ash, Liz, and Alex. They all did not want this to happen. It was better to play it safe. "Why do you even want to do this, Mimi?" asked Kendall. "Just yesterday, you were depressed and practically suicidal, and now, you want to put everyone else's life in danger as well. You all could get killed!"

"I'm not trying to kill anyone! This law doesn't affect people like Ms. Jane and David, but yet, there are still thousands just like them who are willing to risk their own life for us, and we are just sitting around doing nothing." Kendall got quiet.

"We need to stay safe, otherwise, their lives would mean nothing," Liz said.

"We will."

"You don't know that." Ash was already mad that Jackson was going.

"As much as I hate this idea, we already chose to go. We are doing it no matter what," Alex defended me.

"Fine," said Ash, "but if anything happens to anyone, I'm blaming you, Mimi." She glared at me. I had never seen her give anyone that look, let alone her best friend. I didn't know what to say or do. Everyone left my room except Britt.

"She doesn't want to see anyone get hurt," said Britt, "and she knows that Alex will protect you regardless."

"I've never seen her that mad though. I'm just not used to her acting this way, and Liz is taking her side. She isn't even sleeping in our room anymore."

"I'll sleep in here tonight. Don't worry too much, okay?" she said. "We all chose to go, so she can't just blame you if something happens. I'm sure this will blow over tomorrow."

"I hope so." We both got into bed. "Do you think something will happen? Do you think someone will end up getting hurt?" Maybe Ash and Kendall were right. I was subconsciously self-inflicting death on everyone. I wasn't meaning too. I didn't want to see anyone of us get hurt.

"I honestly don't know," she said. "I know you don't want any of us to get hurt. Don't blame yourself for wanting to fight back. I'm sure the other team would have wanted us to go."

"Do you think they're dead?"

"I don't know."

Chapter 12

"All right, kids," Ms. Jane said. "I'm off to work. I thought I wouldn't have to say this but don't let anyone in the house. Do you understand?" Ms. Jane was tired. She had bags under her eyes. I could see that the stress was getting to her.

"Yes, Ma'am," we all said. She walked out of the kitchen and into the garage. We heard the garage go up, her car leaving, and then, the garage door was shut.

"So what do we do now?" Jackson asked.

Everything had been leading up to this moment. Now, it was Tuesday, and we were about to do the most reckless thing since we had been in this situation.

"Do we have the directions?" I asked Jackson.

"Yes. It isn't far at all."

"Okay, then I think we are good to go." I had to be missing something. "Wait, we need our disguises."

"I have them," Alex said. He came down the stairs with five sweatshirts and sunglasses. I turned to Ash and Liz. They both hadn't talked to me since I advised the plan. Ash was still upset. She spoke to Jackson and Britt though. It bothered Britt that Ash was blaming everything on me, but she tried not to come between anything.

"Well, I guess we are leaving now." I ended. Alex had two gray sweatshirts and a light blue, green, and black one. I took the blue one, and Britt took the green. Both Alex and Henry wore gray while Jackson wore black. Britt got Ash and Liz a hug.

"We will be safe. I promise," Britt told Ash. Ash mumbled something, but I could not understand.

"Be safe," Josh said.

"Don't do anything stupid." Kendall stared directly at me. I didn't enjoy her impudent tone. "Especially you, Mimi." She half grinned. Just a few days ago, she was yelling at me and calling me suicidal, but now, she was smiling at me. I was slightly confused, but I smiled back.

"Don't worry. We will be fine," I said to everyone. I gave Taylor and Perry a hug. I turned to Ash. She acted as if she couldn't see me.

"Okay, I will start hot-wiring the car." Henry walked to the garage.

"We should be back no later than five." I turned around and went into the garage. Britt, Jackson, and Alex followed.

"This might take a while guys," Henry said. "I know how to do it in theory, but I've never actually done it before.

"Great," Britt said. "Just try you're best." She smiled and sat beside him.

"So, should we all stay together?" asked Jackson. "I've been thinking that it will look a little suspicious if we are all together wearing the same exact thing." Jackson had a point.

"Oh, you're right Jackson. We may need to split up," Britt said.

"No, that was not a part of the plan," Alex said. "We stick together. We are safer together." Of course, Alex would feel this way.

"We actually aren't though," I said. "If we stay together, someone will be able to pick us out quicker."

"How about we split into two groups?"

"No."

"Alex, calm down," Henry said, "They make a valid point. We shouldn't drift too far apart though. We break into two groups, but we can see each other at all times."

"That never works. It more than likely will be chaotic there."

"Well, if we can't see each other, then we will go back to the car and then stick together, all right?"

"I like Henry's plan," Britt said.

"Me too."

"Me too!"

"Fine," Alex caved in. "But I stick with Mimi."

"Fine by me." Like I would have agreed to anything else.

"Jackson, Britt, and I will stay near each other," Henry said, and the engine started. "Okay, we have a deal." We got into the car. Henry drove. Jackson sat in the passenger's seat while Britt, Alex, and I sat in the back.

It was a pretty quiet drive besides my heart pounding, and Britt asking how far we were every two seconds. Everyone seemed to be nervous. It was one thing planning it, but now, it was actually happening. I was scared. My heart was pounding through my chest. I thought everyone could hear it.

"You know, guys, this is going to be our first time out of Ms. Jane's house in like six months," Britt pointed out. It was true. We had been hiding in her house for so long that I barely remembered how a McDonald's looked.

"Technically, Mimi and I were the first ones out of the house." Alex winked at me. It had been a while since I had seen him be his somewhat goofy self.

"Oh yeah, two feet outside of the house," Britt said. "Big deal!"

"It actually was a big deal; we smelled flowers, looked at the landscape, pretended we were a couple. It was a pretty awesome time."

"That lasted five minutes. Whatever, now Jackson, Henry and I also get to come outside." It was interesting to watch Britt and Alex talk to one another. I had never seen them interact.

"Congratulations."

"Thank you!" Alex barely ever spoke with my friends. The only person he ever talked to was I, and now, I realized that he and Britt would make great friends. They both can be incredibly annoying, for different reasons, and they both had outgoing personalities—they could have been related.

"Mimi, you're so quiet." Britt decided to join me in the conversation.

"She gets quiet when she's nervous," she continued.

"Maybe she's realizing how dangerous and stupid this plan is," said Alex. Then he had to be rude.

"No need to be snarky with her. Goodness. She is just trying to help end this law. Everyone needs to stop giving her crap about it, especially you and Ash." Britt always defended me.

"It is a dumb plan and could get us all killed. Seriously, why did you guys even agree with her?" He was speaking to Jackson and Henry.

"Because we have a mind that is apparently completely different from yours," Henry said. "She wants to make a difference. You want to play it safe, which is actually surprising. I thought you would be more into the idea."

"He hates the idea because Mimi came up with it. He doesn't want to see her get hurt." *Thank you Britt for making it awkward.* I still wasn't speaking. I started to feel dizzy.

"It's just a stupid plan," Alex said to Britt.

"Right, because you and Henry's plan to figure out if there was some sort of detector on the trail was so much better."

"I remember us all coming up with that idea."

"But you were all for it. This is a well-thought-out plan that we are going to go through."

"Shut up! Everyone just shut up!" I yelled. All the anxiety had to come out of me somehow. Strangely, everyone listened.

"Umm…we're here," Henry said. I looked out the window. There were tons of people out in the streets with signs and shirts saying "Free the Fugitives." Other people were yelling words that I could not completely understand. People were all aligned walking in the same direction forward. Some would turn to different streets to reach to other people. Surprisingly, there weren't any police officers.

"Well, let's park and get out of the car then," Britt said.

"Wait! We have to go over our plan first," said Alex. "Mimi and I stick together while you guys stay behind us. I will be turning around to see you guys every five minutes. Y'all do the same. If we don't see each other, then we go straight to the car."

"That's fine," Jackson said. Henry was looking for somewhere to park. So many cars were parked across the street where signs specifically said No Parking.

"Where do I park?" asked Henry.

"Just find a place to park off the side of the road like the other cars," Britt responded.

"It says No Parking."

"Just do it."

He drove on the street till he found a parking spot. "I don't know if I can parallel park."

"Try." I wasn't driving yet so I couldn't give an opinion. I closed my eyes hoping he would not bump into any cars.

"Stop! You're about to hit that car," said Britt. "Here, let me get out." Britt couldn't drive either. I didn't understand how she knew what to do. She got out of the car and stood on the walkway. She told him to go forward. Then she would tell him to stop, turn his steering wheel and go in reverse. He would do it. Then she told him to go forward again. He finally got in.

"Thanks," Henry said.

"How did you know how to park?" I was confused.

"I'm fifteen, Mimi! I have a permit now, and I've been practicing with my parents." I forgot about that. We were all out of the car.

"Remember," Alex said. "We meet here."

"Got it," Jackson responded. "Be safe guys."

"You too." Alex grabbed my hand, and we walked off. There were tons of people next to me yelling with signs. All of these people reminded me of Layla. There energy, ambition, and hope was as strong as hers. I could never get her excited face out of my head. I saw parked cars from around the country: Georgia, Florida, Tennessee, Virginia, and Texas. There were probably even more cars from even more states.

"There are so many people." I looked at Alex.

"I know."

"Should we be yelling?" I asked. "We look out for place without signs."

"I think we should try to keep as much attention off of us as possible."

"We would do that if we yelled."

Alex paused and then yelled; "Free the fugitives! Yeah!" He yelled off the top of his lungs. He turned to me. "Happy?"

I laughed. "Very."

He smiled at me. I missed his smile. I would always lose it. One day, I would see it, but then his smile would go away, and if I was lucky, I would see it again after a week. I put him through a lot. All of the ideas I created in my head were stupid to him, and they always got everyone in trouble or risked our lives.

"I'm sorry," I said.

"For what?"

"For making you come here. This idea was obviously stupid to you and everyone who chose to stayed at home. I shouldn't have put everyone in danger, and last week, I put everyone in danger when Mrs. Wilson caught me spying on her and for—" He interrupted me.

"Mimi. Don't apologize. It's not your fault. I chose to come here. You didn't make me. Don't feel guilty for that."

"Then why do you get so irritated when I come up with an idea or screw up?"

"Because the thought of you getting hurt upsets me." I didn't know what to say. I wasn't expecting that. It just made me remember all of the things he said when Mrs. Wilson was there.

"Last week with Mrs. Wilson, you said a lot of things." I wasn't sure if I wanted to know the answer to the question I was about to ask. He looked down. I felt like he didn't want to talk about it, and maybe, I didn't either. Not right now at least. I turned around and saw Jackson. Britt waved at me.

"Go on," he said. Maybe he did want to talk about it, but I didn't even know what to say.

"Well—"

Someone interrupted me, "I know you!"

He was walking towards Alex and me. He was tall with short brown hair. He had a friend with him who was much shorter. I didn't recognize them, so I didn't understand how they knew me. Alex grabbed my hand a little tighter.

"Who are you?" he said in a stern manner.

"My name is Bailey, and this is my friend Mathew." Matt smiled and continued to stare at Alex and I in awe.

"How do you know who we are?" I asked.

"You guys are the fugitives."

My heart stopped. We were already picked out. I knew this was a bad idea.

"You're Mimi, and you're Alex," Mathew said.

They even knew our names. This was insane. I didn't even know what to say.

"No, we're not! Ha! We are just supporting the cause," lied Alex.

"No need to lie. We're on your side," Bailey said. "We think what they're doing to you guys is horrible and unconstitutional. It is worse in the south. Too many conservatives I suppose."

They looked a bit older, possibly college students.

"Where are you guys from?" I asked.

"Well, I'm from Alabama," Bailey said, "but my friend is from New York. We go to Columbia University. I came down here to visit my family, and Mathew had nothing interesting to do this fall break, so he decided to join. We heard about the march and decided to attend."

"We never would have thought we would meet you guys here," Matt said. "You have no idea how many students protest in New York."

"We've been in hiding. We don't know what is going on politically. Have they overturned this law?" Alex asked.

"Not yet. Congress and the Supreme Court have been debating it for weeks now. They're getting closer to a solution," Bailey told us.

"What do you think is going to happen?" I asked.

"Honestly," Matthew said, "I believe that this will be resolved in the next month or two, maybe less. It's contingent on how chaotic citizens continue to get. There have been riots where citizens were injured. That outraged a good amount of people."

"This didn't scare you guys into coming?"

"No," said Bailey. "This is just a march. It seems more reserved than the ones I've seen on the news. I expected more commotion than this. I don't see too many police officers." He seemed to be enjoying himself. Both of them did. They liked being united with people who all wanted the same thing: change. That was part of the reason I wanted to come here. Knowing that people were here to end this law and joining them was an amazing feeling.

"This is unconstitutional!" they both yelled.

"Thank you," I said.

"For what?"

"For caring. It means a lot."

They looked at me and smiled.

All of a sudden I heard it. Everyone's yells instantly turned to screams, and people began to turn around and run. I heard another one. Only this time it was pointed towards the person beside me. I screamed.

"Matt!" Bailey grabbed his friend. He had been shot. Blood was dripping from his chest.

"Mimi, we have to go and find everyone."

I was still. I couldn't move. I just stared at Bailey and Mathew. They were covered with blood, and Mathew was dying. Someone who wasn't supposed to die was dying because of this law. Alex grabbed me and ran. We ran back to the car. We could see blood trailing towards it. I looked up and saw Jackson.

"Oh my goodness!"

He was bleeding in the arm.

"I am so sorry. This is all my fault."

"I'm fine, Mimi. I just need to get this bullet out of my freaking arm. It burns like hell!"

I continued to hear more gunshots.

"We need to get in the car and go now," Alex demanded. He opened the door and put Britt and me in the car. "I don't care if you hit a car, just get us out of here," Alex said to Henry as he started driving. People were running across the streets trying not to get hurt. Fights were starting. It was anarchic. I couldn't help to think of Bailey and Mathew, if they were okay or not. Now, someone was injured because of me.

"I'm so sorry! I did this," I said.

"Seriously, I'm fine! I just need to get this bullet out and maybe some stitches."

"You're still hurt! It's my entire fault. I should have never come up with this idea. It was a stupid plan. Why on earth would I decide to risk our lives for this? There was no point!" I was still crying. The image of that boy getting shot played in my mind over and over again, and now, he was dead. He was just a college student. He hadn't gotten the chance to get married or start a family.

"It's okay, Mimi. He isn't dead," Britt said. "He is alive."

"People are dying out there! I just witnessed a man get shot in the chest right in front of me. He was only in college, and he was shot right in the chest. I'm sure he wasn't the only one."

Britt didn't know what to say. She just held me as I cried.

"That bullet needs to come out," Alex told Jackson.

"I think you should leave it in there until someone sees it. It could be stopping you from bleeding," Henry said.

"You might be right," Alex said.

I didn't understand how he was acting this way. Someone died in front of us.

"How are you so calm right now?" I couldn't tell if he understood me with all of my crying.

"Someone has to be," he said.

I left it at that. There was no point in getting into an argument about it. I closed my eyes, hoping this was just a nightmare. I opened my eyes. Unfortunately, it was my reality; I closed them again, only to picture my mother.

"I told you that pie is your desert, not your dinner!" my mom said. There was a key lime pie sitting on the kitchen counter. My mother bought it from Walmart. Since she worked there, she could randomly get discounts. Food was never a problem in my household, nor were clothes. My mother dreaded college though. She created a college fund for me and prayed that one day I would be able to get into a good school, and she would be able to afford it.

"Mom, calm down. Like you weren't about to get a piece yourself."

She laughed. There was a pizza in the oven. She always got the vegetarian pizza because she wanted to stay somewhat healthy while eating a pizza full of grease.

"Hey. The rules are different for me. I get to eat whatever I want. You on the other hand follow by my rules."

"Yes, ma'am."

"So how is school going along?"

"It's good. Ninth grade isn't that hard. I have pretty good teachers too. There not that bad."

"Keep up the good work. You only have three more years until you're in college. I want you to go to a good school and get the education I never had. I don't want you to live like me."

"What's wrong with the way we live?"

"Nothing sweetie. It's just very limited. I want you to be able to become whatever you want. I want you to be able to provide more for the family you will have someday."

"Well, I think you're doing a great, Mom."

"Aw gee, thanks darling."

She pinched my cheeks and laughed. My mother always laughed. She was a happy mother, and definitely, one of the most beautiful persons I knew. She never wanted me to see how much she hurt. It was just she and I. I was all she had, and even though it was all I knew, I could tell she was frustrated sometimes. She didn't show me just how frustrated, but I knew she was. I knew our lifestyle bothered her. I knew she wanted more for us, and I could tell she regretted her life every day. "So are there any boys you like at school?"

"Ha. No, Mom."

There was no one I was ever interested in. There were guys I was friends with, but nothing more than that. I was only fourteen.

"Seriously?" She was surprised. "Well, I guess that's a good thing. You shouldn't be dating at your age."

I just didn't like anyone.

"I have to go to work early tomorrow. Don't let anyone in the house, okay? If someone knocks, you ignore, all right?"

"Why would I open the door to a stranger?"

"You might be thinking it's one of your friends, I don't know. Just make sure you don't do it, all right?"

"Okay, Mom."

"I think the pizza is ready!"

Chapter 13

"Mimi, we're home," Britt said. All of a sudden, I was jerking. Someone was shaking me, and I didn't know what to do. I wasn't with my mom anymore. It was just a memory I relived in a dream. The last one I had.

"Ms. Jane is home," Henry said.

"We are going to be in trouble," Britt responded.

"Ow. It still burns." Jackson stared at his arm.

We all got out of the car and walked to the door. I was at first terrified to open it—but I did anyway. It was quiet at first. Maybe, this was the dream, and being with my mom was the reality. I couldn't stand being in this house; it was too quiet. I walked into the kitchen. Everyone was in the kitchen, and once they saw us, it was like the march all over again.

"Why don't you ever listen to me?" I could hear the anger in Ms. Jane's voice.

"Oh my gosh! Jackson!" Ash immediately noticed his arm.

"It's all over the news. There are videos of you guys there! They know we are hiding in Alabama!" Liz had to tell us what we already thought.

"You got your wish, Mimi! We're all dead now!" Kendall was upset.

"I told you that if anyone got hurt I was blaming you! You're dead to me!" Not as much as Ash.

"I can't protect you anymore!" Everyone was silent once Ms. Jane said that.

"What do you mean?" I asked.

"You're not safe here. It isn't safe for you guys to be here anymore. It will be a matter of time before they find out where you guys are. You have to relocate somewhere else."

"This is all your fault, Mimi." Ash completely despised me. I had never seen her full with so much hatred for anyone, let alone me. The doorbell rang.

"That is probably David?" Ms. Jane opened the door. It was Mrs. Wilson.

"I knew it this entire time! You were fugitives, and there are more of you! I'm calling the police right now."

I didn't understand why she felt the need to come to the house before she called the police. We could have just tied her down and held her hostage.

"We have pictures of you cheating on your husband. If you really want to so continue living in that beautiful little house of yours, I suggest you don't call anyone," Jackson said. He pulled the out from his pocket and showed it to her. This really was insurance.

She gave him a death stare. "Are you blackmailing me?"

"Yes, we are. Now, please leave."

"There is no way I'm letting you get away with this. You're all supposed to be dead! You all deserve to be dead."

All of a sudden Perry, Taylor, and Emily appeared.

"Hi, our name is Taylor. Her name is Emily and that's Perry. What's yours?" They all smiled.

"My name is Mrs. Wilson. How old are you girls?" She seemed to be somewhat sympathetic towards the little girls.

"I'm ten, she's eleven, and she is nine."

Mrs. Wilson stared at them intensely. For a split second, I saw compassion in her eyes. I didn't think that was possible. "Okay fine, I won't call the police, but it will be a matter of time before the police find y'all. Be safe." As she turned around to leave, David came in. He looked at all of us in regret and despair. I knew he was upset with all of us. He saw Jackson's arm. "What happened?"

"I was shot."

"We need to get that fixed now." He turned to Ms. Jane. "I'm going to go upstairs to try and get the bullet out."

"Do you know what you're doing?" Ash asked. She was worried about Jackson.

"Yes. I do. Come on, kid." He took Jackson with him. Now, it was everyone and Ms. Jane who didn't even know what to say to any of us. She was disappointed in everyone and couldn't believe what we had done. I put everyone's life in danger as they tagged along.

"I'm so sorry, Ms. Jane." That was all I could do.

"Me too." That was all she could say. She looked at Alex. "I guess we're going to have to postpone your trip."

"What is she talking about, Alex?"

"Ms. Jane was going to try and contact my aunt and see if I could meet her."

It all made sense now. That was what they were discussing last week. He was supposed to meet his aunt, and I ruined it. My stupid, irrational plan ruined everything. Jackson was injured, we had to leave Ms. Jane 's home, Alex couldn't meet his only living relative, and everyone else pretty much hated me. I didn't even know why I wanted to go anymore. Maybe it was just out of boredom. Maybe I was just tired of being in the house all the time, and I wanted to do something different, but my boredom has put everyone in danger, and it wasn't fair to anyone.

"I didn't mean for any of this to happen."

"It's okay, Mimi."

"No, it's not! You risked all of our lives!" Kendall was angry.

"Now, we don't have anywhere to hide. Now, we are practically dead! You ruined everything you touch, Mimi!" Ash was even angrier.

"Ash, calm down. We chose to go. Stop trying to blame everything on her," Britt defended me.

"How can you stand up for her? She has ruined your life," Ash said. "She is the reason you're here. Because of her, Jackson is upstairs getting a bullet pulled out of his arm, we all have to find another place to stay, and Alex can't meet his aunt anymore."

"If you want to blame someone, then look in the mirror. You could have worked harder to stop us, but you didn't. Hell, you could have even told Ms. Jane, and none of this would've happened, so stop blaming it on Mimi."

Ash was silent.

"Oh," continued Britt, "and I stand up for her because she is my friend. We have all been close since we were in elementary school. We are all friends, or did you forget?" She didn't bother to say anything else. That subject was closed.

"So what are we doing now?" Chase asked.

"We wait until David comes back down and tells you guys where you're going," Ms. Jane said.

"Why can't we just stay here? Sure they know we are in Alabama, but it's not like they know exactly where we are," Andrew said.

"There were tons of witnesses that saw them. Someone could have seen the car they went into. All the police have to do is see how many citizens own the particular car and narrow it down. They could find you in a matter of days, maybe even hours. That is why you guys have to find somewhere else to hide."

"What are you going to do if police show up?" John asked.

"Well, if y'all are gone, then I should be fine. They might want to come in and check the house, so I will have to straighten everything out, but that is about it. I doubt they will have any evidence that traces me to you."

"Okay," David said, "so we have some good news, bad news, and worse news." He came down the stairs with Jackson. His arm was wrapped, but he seemed fine. "The good news is that the march actually rallied up more citizens, and the government is leaning towards overruling the law. Since thirty people were injured, and six were found dead, and there have been other marches with similar outputs, I believe this law will end within a few weeks, possibly less. The bad news is that you all have been spotted, and there are tons of witnesses that will speak out. If you stay here, you will die. I have a charter bus in the driveway to take you."

"So what's the worse news?" Henry asked.

"I have no idea where you can stay."

We were screwed.

"What!" Ms. Jane flipped. "Why can't they stay with you?"

"Do you know how suspicious that will be? I'm a double agent, and besides, I live in a one-bedroom apartment. There isn't any space."

We were completely screwed.

"Do you not know anyone they can stay with?"

"Not that I trust. Do you?"

Ms. Jane thought. "Everyone I know either supports the law or is indifferent. There is no way I could trust them to keep these kids safe."

"We could go back to my home. It can fit fifteen people." Britt volunteered.

"Your parents are more than likely being watched. There phones are probably bugged and everything. That will be too risky," David said.

"Well, we don't have another choice," Britt said.

"We might," Ms. Jane said.

"What?"

"You could stay at Alex's aunt's house. She lives in Atlanta. I can give you her address."

"Do you trust her?" David asked.

"I doubt she will let her nephew die."

"But will she take all of them?"

"You will have to be very convincing. Explain everything to her. If she still isn't convinced, then show her the little girls. We should definitely get a sympathy vote."

"Are you sure she will even take me? She put me up for adoption. How are you so sure she will take me now?"

"I already spoke with her. She seemed interested enough to see you. She was quiet, but I could tell she cared."

"Are you sure this is a good idea?" David asked.

"No, but it's the best plan we have."

We were desperate, and there was nothing else we could do.

"Well, Atlanta is a little less than three hours away, so if we leave now, then we should be able to get there by ten."

"Okay, everyone pack at least five shirts and shorts, and you might want to take the covers off of the bed too!"

"We don't have suitcases?"

"I recycle grocery bags. They're all in the utility room. Now get packing!" she yelled.

I went to the utility room and got two grocery bags. I went to my room. Liz was in the room getting her clothes. She still wasn't talking to me. I got my clothes and toothbrush and took one of the covers off of the bed. Liz had already taken the comforter. She walked out of the room without saying anything to me. I looked around the room I had spent six months in. I remembered the first day I was in here. I was hurt, and Alex carried me in here. I remembered all the times Britt, Liz, Ash, and I talked and laughed. We laughed during the darkest period of our lives, and we became closer and stronger out of it. Maybe I was wrong. Maybe we weren't any stronger than our first day here, but I was going to miss this place. It was a home for me.

"Hey. Everyone is down. We have to leave soon." It was Alex.

"Are you going to be okay?" I didn't know how he felt about meeting his aunt for the first time.

"As long as we're alive, I'll be fine."

"How do you feel about meeting your aunt?"

"I don't know. I'm not expecting too much."

"Well, I'm here for you."

"I know. Everyone hates you now, so I'm the only person you have to talk to," he laughed.

"Shut up!"

"Too soon?"

"Yes!"

"Your friends are just mad right now. Trust me, they will forgive you."

"Thanks."

"As long as you stop risking our lives all the time."

I hit him while he laughed. "You are such a jerk. You do realize that?"

"You love it."

I smiled. After everything that happened, I almost hated the fact that Alex was making me smile. It didn't feel right. I had watched someone die right in front of my eyes. I felt guilty. It wasn't fair for him to have died for our cause, while we escaped and still were safe. "We had fun here, didn't we?"

"About as much fun as a fugitive can have."

"I'll still miss it."

"Me too."

I didn't want to say good-bye to this room or to Ms. Jane. She protected us in a time when we needed a savior. I repaid her by disobeying her constantly when she knew what was right for me.

"Well, we have to go now." I wrapped two bags around my shoulder. Alex grabbed my hand. We walked out of the room and down the main staircase. Ms. Jane was crying. There were tears pouring down her face. She was hugging everyone.

"Be safe," she said to all of us. Everyone started departing. Ms. Jane gave me a huge hug. "You have a good heart."

"I'm so sorry."

"I understand why you went. I probably would have done the same. You felt guilty. I understand."

"Thank you so much for everything." Tears started to fall down my faces and unto my neck.

"Promise me you will be more careful."

"I promise."

She hugged me. "Take care of Alex. He will need you," she whispered in my ear.

"Of course I will."

"I know Mimi hunny." She was still crying. She hugged Alex and said goodbye. We went outside and walked towards the bus. I turned around, and Ms. Jane was still waving at us.

"Are you ready?" Alex asked.

"Are you?"

We got onto the bus and left.

Chapter 14

It was silent during the ride to Atlanta. Most people were sleeping while others were wishing they were asleep—I wished. I could tell Alex was anxious about meeting his aunt for the first time, especially under these circumstances. He didn't know what to expect: was she going to let him in while also letting fourteen other children in? The odds weren't very high. I was especially nervous for him because I knew he was worried. Besides, if she didn't let us in, we had nowhere else to go.

"Okay," David said. "It looks like she lives in a condo."

I looked out the window. We were entering an apartment complex. There was no way she would have enough room for us in an apartment. This was not going to work out. I already knew it. I looked over at Alex. I could see he was thinking the same thing. David stopped the bus. "Okay, so I was thinking we bombard her." That sounded like the worst idea ever.

"I don't think that's a good idea," Alex said.

"We don't really have a choice," he went on. "I was thinking that everyone stay behind me, except Alex.

We introduce her to Alex first. Then we explain everything. Maybe that will be the best way to handle this."

It did not sound like the best way to handle this at all, but I didn't know what to do.

"Okay."

"All right then, let's go."

Everyone got out of the bus. We followed David, since he knew what her apartment number was. He stopped in front of a door. "Okay, everyone else step back."

We all moved about four steps back. He knocked on her door. There was no response. I wasn't surprised. It had to be ten at night, and she could have been out doing something. David knocked again. There was still no response.

"What if she isn't here?" Alex asked.

"She will be." He knocked again. Someone answered the door.

"What on earth do you want?"

I couldn't see her. We were farther back, but I could hear her speaking.

"Hello, Ms. Koneru. My name is David, and this is Alex."

It was quiet. I was sure she recognized him. She had to know who he was.

"What are you doing here?" she asked.

"We have a problem. I'm sure Ms. Jane informed you on the circumstances we are under, right?"

"No, I do not believe she did."

"Oh. Well, I'm sure you watch the news. You are aware of the Children's Act that has been passed right?" David whispered.

"Yes, it's a horrible law. What does...?"

I could tell from her tone that she understood now.

"Well, right now. He doesn't have anywhere else to go. The police found out where he was hiding, and we had to flee. He needs somewhere to stay."

"You want me to foster a fugitive? I can't do that right now. I have a job. Is there anywhere else he can stay?"

"No, I'm afraid not. Staying anywhere else would be a danger to him. The police will never think to check here."

"And if they do?"

"This law should be ending soon. After the march in Birmingham, everything should be turning back to normal within a few weeks, maybe less."

It was silent again for a while.

"Okay, I will do it."

"There's a catch."

"Go on."

"Well, Alex was a part of a group of fugitives."

"How many?"

"Fourteen others."

"You want me to house fifteen kids! Are you delirious?" she yelled.

"Ma'am, if you do not, they will die. They have nowhere else to go."

"And exactly, why can't you take care of them?"

"Because I work for the government. It would be too dangerous for them to stay with me, and I also live in

Birmingham, which is exactly where they were caught. The safest place is with you."

"I live in a three-bedroom condo! I have neighbors that are a wall apart from me. I can't do this."

"If you don't, we're dead, and I doubt you want to feel the guilt for the death of fifteen children." It was the first thing Alex said to her. She still was silent.

"Fine, but they have to be completely quiet. I cannot have too much commotion going on in this complex."

"Thank you so much. All right, kids you can come in."

I walked towards her door and saw her. She was young, but tired. She had dark skin with dark hair and dark eyes to go along with it. A part of me already envied her beauty. She looked astonished but not angry.

"Okay well, I can help you get settled in," David offered.

Her living space was the size of a box compared to Ms. Jane's, but it was still nice and spacious. When you walked in, there was the living area and the kitchen. That was all I saw at first, but as I continued to walk in, I saw a staircase. It was a huge condo. I had never seen anything like it.

"Okay well, I only have two other bedrooms, so all girls in one, and all boys in the other. Most of you seem old enough to organize the sleeping arrangements for yourself. I don't want to hear anyone talking till three in the morning. My bedroom is not too far from yours. This house only consists of two bathrooms, so all of you will have to share a bathroom. Don't go into my bathroom and do not mess with any of my things. You are welcome to the kitchen, but you have to clean up after yourself. I am not your mother. Is everything clear?"

No one responded.

"All right, that is all for now. We can discuss everything else in the morning." She didn't look at Alex. I could tell it was affecting him.

"Okay well," David said, "I guess she told you guys everything. I need to head back to Alabama, so I have to go." He looked at Ms. Koneru. "I will be calling you as soon as this ends. It should not take any more than three weeks. I honestly believe this visit will only last a week."

"Okay."

"Good night, everyone." David was gone. Now, it was just her taking care of us. I could see she was incredibly tired.

"Well, I might just go off to bed. We will talk about everything in the morning." She looked at Alex. "Good night." She headed up the stairs as we followed her to our other rooms. She at first was confused, but then realized she didn't tell us where the rooms were. "Girls, you should probably sleep in that one because there is more space, and there are more of you. Guys, the other bedroom is down the hall." She went to her room, which was directly in the center. I opened the door to our room. It was pretty big but not as large as the one in Ms. Jane's house.

"Okay, so I was thinking three in the bed, and everyone else on the floor. We can alternate who gets to sleep on the floor each night," I suggested.

"Me, Liz, and Kendall will sleep on the bed and you two can sleep on the floor with the children," Ash said. She was still mad at me.

"Sounds fine to me," Britt said. She and I started to create a bed with our sheets and the children's sheets. I actually sort of liked sleeping on the floor. Whenever I would have extended family over at my house, I would have to sleep on the floor, and it was always comfortable to me.

"I think we should go to sleep soon," Ash said. "We need to respect her t."

"I agree," Kendall said.

"Let's try not to get anyone shot this time." Ash was still going on about it. I just ignored her. Part of her was right. It was entirely my fault. I was the reason Jackson was shot, and I had to take responsibility for my actions. Jackson was able to forgive me, and I wished Ash were too.

"Enough, Ash," Britt said.

"Jackson was almost killed, and you want me to calm down!"

"Yes!"

"How about you stop talking for her! She can speak for herself!"

I looked at her. "I'm sorry. I know it was my fault, and I feel completely guilty for everything that has happened—"

"Shut up, Mimi, it's not your fault," Britt interrupted me. "Look, Ash, as I said earlier, you could have stopped this if you really wanted to, but you didn't. She might have created the idea, but we didn't have to go along with it. None of us stopped her, therefore it is our fault as well."

"Jackson almost died."

"Ash, we have been on the run for months now. Every day we are alive is a blessing. Now, please be grateful that Jackson only 'almost' died. He is still alive."

Ash was quiet.

"You guys should really stop arguing," Kendall joined in. "I mean, I'm upset too, but Britt has a point. We can't just blame everything on Mimi. We didn't try to stop her, and we need to be thankful that we all are still alive after everything we have been through."

That might have been one of the nicest things Kendall had ever said to me, even though it wasn't completely directed towards me.

"I am grateful, okay. It's just going to take me some time to forgive her for this. I still blame you, Mimi, and I don't know if I will ever be able to forgive you."

I was shattered.

"I understand." I walked out of the room. I didn't know where I was going but the tension was too much. I didn't want to wake up Alex's aunt up, so I quietly went downstairs. I saw Alex in the kitchen getting a drink of water.

"How are you?"

He turned around and saw me. "I don't know."

"I'm so sorry, Alex. This is all my fault. You shouldn't have had to meet your aunt under these circumstances."

"This isn't your fault, it's our fault."

I gave him a subtle smile. I knew he was just trying to make me feel better about ruining everyone's life even more than it already was. Jackson might have been the one shot, but he was fine. I had screwed up Alex the most even though he won't admit it.

"I'm glad your aunt let us stay here."

"Yeah."

"How do you feel about her?"

"I don't know. She would barely even look at me today."

"I think there are a lot of things she wants to say to you, but they're personal. I'm sure she has an understanding of what you might be thinking. She wants to explain everything when you guys can talk about it alone. Plus, she was really tired. Who in their right mind would have let us stay with them then go to sleep right after we get here?"

Alex laughed. "Yeah, I guess you're right."

I could tell he was still bothered.

"Hey." I got closer to him and wrapped my arms around his shoulders. "I know you can get through this." I stood on my toes to kiss him on the cheek. "I know you will."

Chapter 15

The light from the window woke us all up. I never noticed that she didn't have any shutters or blinds to keep people from seeing us. I went to the bathroom so I could be the first one in there. I brushed my teeth and washed my face before anyone else was awake. Suddenly, I saw Jackson.

"I'm surprised you're awake," I told him. "You are usually the last person to wake up."

"Well, yesterday was a long day, and I was ready to start the next I suppose." Jackson started brushing his teeth.

"How is your arm?"

"It still stings a little, but I'm fine."

I didn't understand how he was taking this so well. He was taking this better than anyone.

"I'm so—"

"Mimi, it's fine. Really. It wasn't your fault."

I felt like I was bugging everyone by apologizing. I just ended that conversation.

"Do you think Ms. Koneru is awake?" I asked.

"I don't know. I passed by her room, and it didn't sound like anyone was in there."

"Do you think she left us here?"

"I doubt that."

I left the bathroom and went downstairs to the kitchen. Ms. Koneru was down there by herself drinking coffee.

"Good morning, Ms. Koneru." I had no idea what else to say to her. It seemed appropriate. She looked up. She looked much more refreshed today and even prettier. I now understood why Alex was so attractive.

"Hello…I'm sorry I don't know your name." She seemed polite.

"My name is Meredith, but everyone calls me Mimi."

"Which one do you prefer?"

"Mimi, I guess."

"Well, good morning, Mimi. I would assume you're hungry. The only food I really have right now are bagels and toast. There is some yogurt in the fridge if you would prefer that. I hope I have enough for fifteen people."

I looked in her fridge and saw some yogurt. She had blueberry, pineapple, lemon, and strawberry-flavored yogurt. I chose the blueberry.

"This looks like enough for today. Thank you so much for letting us stay at your house."

"It was the least I could do."

I didn't believe her. It was definitely more than she could have done.

"How did you sleep?" she asked.

"I slept well, and you?"

"It was sleep, so I can't complain." She smiled.

"Do you have a busy work schedule?" I asked.

"Sort of. I'm a radiologist."

All I knew about radiologists was that they made a lot of money. If she was making so much money, then why would she have to leave Alex?

"So you have a job that pays really well."

"You're wondering why I left him. I think I should probably talk to Alex about that, but just know that I was really young. If I had taken care of him, then I would not be where I am today. I would not have been able to give him the best life possible. That is why he was adopted into a family that was supposed to provide for him."

"Yeah, well, look where we are now."

"Oh, the irony."

"I don't mean to be rude Ms. Koneru, but after this is over, Alex has nowhere to go. You can't let him return to his adopted parents. He deserves better than that."

She looked at me. "I'm beginning to realize that."

All of a sudden, I heard someone coming down the stairs. It was Jackson.

"Good morning."

"Good morning, Ms. Koneru. My name is Jackson."

"What happened to your arm?"

"I was shot, but I am perfectly fine." Jackson emphasized on the "fine" part while staring at me.

"Would you like any breakfast?"

"Yes."

He saw the bagels and put one in the toaster. "Everyone should be coming down soon."

"Good, I want to talk to all of you."

We waited in awkward silence. Eventually, people started to come down. I saw Josh, Chase, Andrew, John, Kendall, Henry, and Britt come downstairs. They all greeted Ms. Koneru. Then I saw, Liz, Ash, and Jason come down. Ash ignored me of course. Eventually, I saw the little kids and Alex come down. Alex stood right beside me but did not stare at his aunt at all.

"Is this everyone?" she asked. We all nodded. "Well, my name is Sara Koneru. I called in sick for work today to get all of you guys adjusted. I'm sure it is hard being so far from your families, and I'm truly sorry for what all of you are going through. Your safety is the most important thing right now, and as David said, this should be blowing over soon. Now, I have a few rules. I spoke with Ms. Jane earlier this morning, and I realized I should probably state the obvious. You will not leave this condo, you are not even allowed to stare outside the window for too long. You will not speak loudly. I understand Ms. Jane lived in decent-sized home, but this is a condo. My neighbor is a wall away. It is essential that you remain quiet. There are fifteen of you, which means a little noise can go a long way. After today, I will have to go to work. When I am gone, I trust you to be on your best behavior. If someone knocks on the door, you do not answer. Act as a ghost. You need to understand that now, my life is at risk as well. Does everyone understand?"

We all nodded our heads.

"We will not make the same mistakes we made with Ms. Jane with you," Britt said.

"I don't think you will. I'm sure having to leave her house was almost like being kidnapped all over again. You were with her for six months, and I know you guys became attached to her. Hopefully, this stay with me will be temporary. I don't have that much food for you guys to eat right now. There are bagels, toast and yogurt. I might actually have some cereal in the pantry. You are all welcome to eat."

"Thank you," Henry said. "We are all truly grateful."

She smiled and said, "Alex, may I speak with you upstairs?"

"Sure."

I was worried of what was going to happen. They went upstairs.

"Well," Britt said, "I doubt we will be getting pancakes and waffles everyday with this lady."

"At least it's food," Chase added.

"True."

We ate in silence. I felt like many of us were trying to adjust to this new house. The children ate at the kitchen table while the rest of us stood. Once we were done, we were too scared to go upstairs because Alex and her aunt were still up there.

"So are we supposed to stay down here?" Kendall asked.

"Until they finished talking, yes," I said.

Kendall walked into the living room and turned on the TV. It was on the news.

"I do not feel like watching this." She changed the channel to something else. Some TV show was on. "Oh my gosh, I love this show!" She sat on the couch and started to watch it. I had no idea what it was, but I sat on the couch next to her. There was nothing else to do. Everyone else migrated to the living room.

"This show is awesome," Jason said.

I didn't even realize how Jason sounded. He rarely even spoke.

"What is it about?" I asked.

"This time traveler who travels through space and time with his companions and sonic screwdriver."

It didn't really sound all that interesting, but I continued to watch it.

"It is the best show on television!" Jason said. He was getting really into the show.

"I know right!" Kendall agreed. After an episode, it seemed pretty interesting, but then, another episode came on. Finally, Alex and Serena came downstairs.

"Sorry, we were up there so long."

"It's totally fine!" Kendall said with excitement. She was so excited to be watching this series. "I found a marathon of my favorite show, so I am satisfied."

Ms. Koneru smiled. Everyone made room for Alex to sit by me. It was almost as if people expected us to be a couple, but I was satisfied nonetheless.

"How was it?" I whispered to him.

"It was all right. She just explained everything to me. I'll tell you everything later."

"We can talk about it now if you want."

"Nah. I would rather sit down and watch television with you, for now." He smiled and held my hand. I didn't know what we were now. It sure felt like we were together, but I wasn't going to ask. I didn't want to worry about that or anything else for that matter. I just wanted to relax with everyone for what was probably the first time since we were kidnapped.

There was an entire marathon of that show, and we watched it until it was time for dinner. Ms. Koneru went out to get us some food. She was gone for maybe thirty minutes. She came back with fried rice and sweet and sour chicken. We all ate in the kitchen together. It was actually really nice. None of us were worrying about everything that had happened before, or even why we were there in the first place. We all talked, bonded, and got to know each other even better. Ash was still hesitant on talking to me, and so was Liz, but at least they were speaking to me in large groups. It was nice to have everyone together. The next day, Ms. Koneru went to work. She seemed to trust us. We pretty much just repeated the same process as we did the day before. We watched television in the living room instead of worrying about when we would have to leave. It was our routine for the next three days.

"Remember when I spoke with my aunt a few days ago?" Alex started out saying.

"Yes."

"Well, she asked me to stay with her when this is all over."

I was so excited for him. I almost attacked him with a hug.

"I'm so happy for you, Alex! This is all wonderful!"

"I know! She has been so nice. She wants me to stay here and live with her."

Then it hit me. He would be staying in Georgia, not Alabama.

"You're staying here," I said,

"Yeah."

I didn't know what to say. "Well, congratulations." I walked away. I knew I was going to start crying if I didn't.

"Wait, Mimi."

I turned around hoping that my eyes would not begin to water. "She told me what you said to her the first day."

I had no idea what he was talking about.

"You told her that I needed to stay with someone, someone that could provide for me."

Now, I remembered. "Well, it was true. You shouldn't be going to your stepparents. They were cruel. You deserve better than that. They didn't even—"

All of a sudden, Alex leaned over and kissed me. It was different than the first time we kissed. It was longer.

"Thank you."

"For what?"

"For everything, for caring about me, for being a genuine friend."

"You don't have to thank me for that."

"Yes, I do."

We went back downstairs. Everyone was watching tv as usual, but it was nice. Alex and I joined in.

"Where have you two been?" Britt asked. She was sitting in between Henry and Josh. I still didn't understand her and Henry's relationship—probably never will.

"Upstairs, weirdo."

"Uh huh." She winked at me. I knew she wasn't spying on me, but somehow, she knew that something happened. We ended up watching the TV until Ms. Koneru was home. For dinner, we had lasagna with garlic bread.

"This is amazing, Ms. Koneru!" I said.

"Don't thank me, thank Stouffer's."

We all laughed. Her cell phone started to ring. She left the kitchen to answer. We couldn't hear anything she was saying.

"Do you think it was David?" I asked everyone.

"Not that soon. He said it would take weeks. It's only been like five days," Britt responded.

"Well, it could be. If he calls, that means this is over. That means we can go home to our families," Kendall said.

"That would be amazing," Jason said. He had been talking much more since we left Ms. Jane's home.

Ms. Koneru came back. "Sorry about that."

"Who was it?" Britt asked.

"David. He says that they have just overruled the law. Ms. Jane is contacting your parents to notify them on your whereabouts. They should be here tomorrow."

Chapter 16

This is what we had all been waiting for, but yet, the room was silent. No one knew what to say or how to react. Our emotions were full of chaotic confusion. I was torn. Part of me was ready to leave and finally see my mother again, but the other part was not ready to let go of everyone.

"Wow," Britt said. There wasn't really much else to say. I honestly was excited that this was finally over. Not just because I would get to see my mother, but the other fugitives would get to see their family who they hadn't seen in a long time. This really was great news, but I felt so incomplete. Don't get me wrong; I was relieved to know that nothing like this would ever happen again. It was officially outlawed and hopefully, history will never repeat itself, but I had grown close to everyone. I was going to miss Liz, Jackson, and even Kendall. These people became my friends, whether I was aware of it or not. I didn't want to end that. I wasn't ready to officially close this chapter—this incredibly tragic chapter, but still a chapter, in my life. I wasn't ready to say good-bye to Alex. I turned to look at him. He was quiet as everyone was, but there was something different about him. There was joy written all over his face. Alex had a family now. He had his aunt to take care of him, and who wouldn't be excited about that? There was no reason for this not to be the most exciting moment of his life; I was honestly happy for him, but it still hurt. I couldn't sit there anymore. I left the kitchen and went up to the room. I wanted to cry, but tears weren't forming, so I just lied on the bed.

"Hey."

I turned around. It was Alex.

"Hey!" I tried to sound perkier, but it wasn't working.

"Are you okay?"

"Of course! I mean, why wouldn't I be? This is great news. We don't have to hide anymore. I get to see my mom! This is what we've all been waiting for: to be free again. That's what we want, right?"

"Right."

He was still concerned for me, but I didn't want him to be. Alex needed to be happy at this time.

"Well then, I am great. I mean, I will miss Henry, Jackson, Liz, Kendall—I will miss everyone, but other than that, I'm pretty excited. It won't be too bad because they will all be in Alabama. I'm just great, really though." And then the tears came running down my face like a waterfall. I wasn't expecting them; they were literal waterfalls coming out of each eye. I covered my face. "I'm just going to miss everyone." I really didn't want him to worry about me. He deserved happiness, especially after everything he went through. I couldn't burden him with my selfish reasons. It wasn't fair.

"Mimi." He sat down beside me and wrapped his arms around my body. "I'm always going to be here."

"I know." I knew that wasn't true. He was almost eighteen, and soon, he was going off to college, and I was fifteen. Now, he lived in a different state. I couldn't expect anything to happen with this. Soon, he was going to forget me, and his feelings would only be a distant memory. As much as he wanted to deny it, it was the truth.

"Look at me."

I stared into his eyes.

"I will always be here. I'm not leaving your life."

"I believe you." I continued to lie. I just wanted to end the conversation as soon as possible.

"You promise?"

"Yes."

He paused for a few seconds and then decided to take it in.

"All right, well, I'm in charge of dishes, so I have to go back downstairs. Do you want to help?

"No, I think I will pack all of my things."

"You don't have anything, but it's okay. You suck at dishes anyway." He winked.

"Oh hush! That's not true at all!" I laughed.

"Right, okay. You can continue believing that." He laughed and walked out. As soon as he left, all the girls that slept in our room walked in.

"Mimi! Are you okay?" Britt asked concerned.

"Ha, I'm fine, Britt."

She didn't believe me. "You may be able to pull this act with Alex, but I've known you too long. What's wrong?" Britt was always so assertive.

"I'm just not ready to say good-bye. I know it sounds stupid and selfish, but a part of me doesn't want to leave tomorrow."

"I don't think any of us are, but I feel like, once you see your mom tomorrow, those feelings will change."

"Maybe."

"You and Alex will keep in touch. Don't worry."

"He's staying here in Atlanta, Britt. He's going to start college soon, so no, I really don't think he is."

"So what if you don't? It isn't the end of the world. If it wasn't meant to be, then it wasn't meant to be," Kendall said. She had a point, but I was wondering if her response was due to jealousy.

"Are you over Alex?" I really couldn't think of any other way to word it.

"I never liked him!"

"That's a lie!" Britt said. "You used to follow him around like a lost puppy. Now, you're a completely different person."

"Okay fine. I did like him, but it was for maybe a few weeks, and it wasn't a lot either. He and Jackson were my only friends here. He was the only person I felt really comfortable around. No offense, but y'all were really cliquish, and I disliked you for it. I was really annoyed by all of you. I'm not going to lie, I mainly did all that Alex stuff to irritate Mimi." That was nice to know. "You were always too scared to talk to him, but it was obvious how much he cared about you. After a while, I just kind of got tired of always talking to Alex, and Jackson would always talk about Ash, so I was just tired."

"I'm sorry we made you feel left out," Ash added.

"I honestly do not care at all."

"So do you think Alex and I will remain close?"

"Ugh. Look, Mimi, how about you discuss this with Alex. Have you ever thought about that?"

"He's so happy right now. I don't want to burden him."

"You wouldn't be a burden and stop worrying about it!"

"I'm just going to miss him so much."

"Just be thankful we are all alive! I'm going to miss you guys, but I am not going to miss all the times you have practically gotten us killed and all the time I spent alone. I value my life, so I'm not going to sit here and be sad about missing y'all. Instead, I'm going to be grateful that my life expectancy has increased. I advise you to do the same."

"It's just so surreal to think," Ash said. "This is over. This is actually over. It's so weird to even say."

"Really though," Liz said. "after everything that has happened, this is how it ends."

"We are done hiding. We are free!" Britt got up and twirled her feet.

"Yeah, we are, and it's freaking awesome," Kendall said. "So let's celebrate."

"Say it loud, 'I'm free, and I'm proud.'" Britt yelled while continuously twirling. Taylor, Perry, and Emily joined her. We all laughed and had a great time like we always did while being here.

"This is our last night being fugitives, guys. What should we do?" I asked.

"You know, I've always wanted to play a prank on the guys," Britt said. It was a great idea.

"Oh my gosh! Yes! Let's do it." I instantly agreed.

"What would we do?" Kendall asked.

"First," Britt said, "we need to check and see if they are asleep."

"There more than likely not," Kendall added.

"Let's check," Liz suggested.

We all got up and left the room, even the little girls.

"We have to be super quiet," Britt said.

"Then hush!" Kendall said.

It was only midnight, so there was no way they were sleeping. We snuck over to the guys' room. I slowly opened the door.

"What are you guys doing?"

I believe it was Chase.

"Nope, there awake. Darn," Britt said in despair.

"What were you guys trying to do? Prank us?" Josh asked?

"Pretty much!" I walked in to the room while everyone followed. Henry was in the bed while every other guy was on the floor with blankets.

"Wow. Henry hogs the entire king-sized bed," I said.

"He's the oldest, so he gets the bed," Alex said.

"Reasonable concept," Britt started. "Guys, this is our last night together! What are we going to do?"

"Sleep," Alex said. Britt frowned. She was expecting us to have a fantastic night and do something exciting, but that wasn't the case. Alex noticed Britt's frown.

"We can't really do anything. We're in a condo, neighbors will hear us, and Sara is trying to sleep, so I don't think that will be a good idea."

"That must be Ms. Koneru's first name. Well, fine, but we can all talk at least. Are you guys excited about finally getting out of this?"

I'm glad to finally see my family, but I will miss you guys," Josh said.

"Aww, so sentimental," Britt said. "I'll miss all of you too."

"Guys, we don't live that far from one another. All of us live in Eufaula or near it. We're going to see each other," Jackson continued.

It was true, all of us lived in Alabama but not Alex. He was staying here, and I wasn't going to see him again. He looked at me, but I turned away.

"I hope no one ever has to go through the same thing we did," I said. "What we've been through is immoral and terrible, but I'm glad I spent it with you. I don't think I could have gotten through this if it weren't for each and every one of you. You all are the reason I'm alive, and I will forever be grateful."

Everyone smiled.

"It's sure been a journey, but I'm ready to leave you guys," Andrew said.

"Andrew, shut up," John responded.

Everyone laughed.

"You don't even know how much I love all of you. I'm really going to miss you guys," Ash said. She looked at Chase, and I and smiled.

I gave her a huge hug. "I love you too!"

"Just know I am never walking to your house again. I don't want some random guy attacking me and throwing me in a car."

"And Mimi, don't open the door to strangers. Check who is at the door, then open it," Britt said.

I laughed. "I can't believe we're actually laughing about this right now." I think most of us were delirious.

"Seriously," Ash said. "whoever thought this would happen?"

I looked around the room. I was saying good-bye to all these people tomorrow, and I think I was ready for most. I would more than likely still see Liz, Jackson, and Kendall. I might even see Henry because of Britt. I still didn't understand their relationship, but oh well.

"Promise we will all keep in touch?" I asked.

"Of course," Alex said.

I knew he believed it, but I doubted his promise.

"We will have reunions every year," Jackson said jokingly.

"That's a great idea!" Britt said. "I'll contact you guys throughout the year."

"All right Britt," Kendall said.

"This is serious. This will be happening every year!"

"I'll make sure of it Brittney," Alex said.

"Deal?"

"Deal."

Chapter 17

Boom. There was a knock on the door. It was time. Time to leave everyone and say good-bye to this part of my life. I was upstairs with Britt and Ash.

"So this is it?" I asked.

"I guess so," Ash said.

"Guys," Britt said, "we all live within five minutes away from one another. I think we will be fine."

"Thanks for ruining the moment, Britt!"

She always had to be so crude. She wasn't nearly as blunt as she used to be. She had grown so much throughout this experience and I was proud of her.

"Sorry," Britt said. She was trying to work on having more consideration for others. "We got through this together, and we are still alive, so I don't think this is it. I think it is the beginning of a new start. Either way, we will still be together." She smiled.

"Is it a bad thing?" Ash asked.

"Is what a bad thing?" Britt responded.

I knew what Ash was referring to.

"Us surviving."

Britt remained quiet. There was nothing you could argue. We got the happy ending, every refugee were not as lucky as we were, so why did we get the happy ending and not them?

"I think one thing that I have learned from this trip is that life isn't fair," I started. "We can't expect everything to be."

"I agree," Britt said while Ash nodded. "There's nothing we can change about the position we are in. I think we should just feel grateful."

"Brittney, Ash, Mimi! Come down stairs!" It sounded like Ms. Jane was the one yelling at us. I didn't realize how much I missed her yelling at us.

"It's time," I said. I looked at Ash and Britt, and we all knew what was on our minds.

"I love all of you," Ash said while hugging us both tightly. We acted as if we were never going to see each other again.

We slowly went downstairs. So many different emotions were spiraling through my body, anxiety, nervousness, and excitement. I turned to look at my mother. A rush of tears fell down my face like an unexpected tsunami. She ran to me as I ran to her. I hugged her as tightly as I could while crying in her arms. I hadn't seen my mother for months, not even realizing that I would ever be able to.

"I missed you so much, Mom"

"I missed you too, Dear." She continued to hold me as if she would never let go. I didn't want to either. I finally had my family back. There was no way I was letting go of that.

"I'm so happy you are safe. Thank the Lord you are safe…I was never for sure if you were. I thought …I thought you."

"I'm right here, Mom. I'm safe."

I turned to see everyone almost having the same conversation with their family. Emily's parents were practically suffocating her, as was Jackson's mom. I turned to look over at Britt. Her parents were full of relief to see their daughter safe. I could tell by Mrs. Palms's expression that she was still upset her daughter was even taken to begin with, however, Mr. Palms was just happy to see his daughter alive.

"Are you ready to go?" my mother asked.

In all honesty I wasn't.

"There are still a few people I have to say goodbye to."

"Okay. I will wait."

I left my mom to find Alex. The house was full of maybe fifty people, all crowded in the living room and kitchen. It was hard to find anyone.

"Mimi!" I heard Ms. Jane yelled.

"Ms. Jane!" I ran to her and gave her a hug. "I really thought I wasn't going to see you again."

"Like I was going to let that happen," she said. "I needed to make sure you guys were safe. Turns out you are."

"Thank you so much for everything. We all wouldn't be alive if it weren't for you."

"It was the humane thing to do."

"I owe you my life, Ms. Jane."

"You don't owe me anything, Mimi, but I want to thank all of you."

We were not exactly the best guests ever.

"For what?"

"I have missed out on a lot of opportunities in my life: marriage and children. Now, I understand the feeling of caring for someone in that way. I want to thank you for that."

I smiled. "It's not too late, you know. David seems like a very nice guy."

"Take care, Mimi."

Ms. Jane was not about to have a conversation over her love life with me. I wasn't really expecting it anyway.

"You too." She turned around and walked away.

I continued to search for Alex. I couldn't see him anywhere. I went up the stairs. He was sitting on the floor. In that moment, I realized I wasn't ready to say goodbye to him.

"Didn't realize you were so antisocial?"

He looked up at me and smiled.

"Watching parents suffocate and cry over their children's well-being," he said. "Not my type of festival."

I sat beside him on the floor. "That's unfortunate. Having your mother squeeze you to death is truly a blast."

He laughed. It was quiet for a while. I didn't know what to say or do. "So are you excited to be staying with your aunt?"

"Yeah," he said. "Actually, we will have so much to talk about after all of you leave."

"Well, that's really good! I'm happy for you." I sincerely was happy, but I just wasn't ready to finally say goodbye.

"Yup."

The conversation was getting incredibly awkward. It was normally very natural to be around him.

"Well, I'm leaving in a few minutes. I just wanted to say good-bye to a few people before I left, so goodbye."

I stood up and reached my hand out for a hand-shake. He got up and shook my hand.

"Bye."

"Bye."

"You already said bye."

"Right."

I was still shaking his hand. He stared at me the same way he did the first time we met. I turned away to leave, but he grabbed my hand closer to him.

"Promise me one thing."

"Yes."

"You will stay in touch."

"Of course."

"I meant every word I said, Mimi."

We had never brought it up. Time just continued to pass before we could.

"I know. I feel the same way."

He kissed my forehead. "I'll see you soon."

"Hopefully."

"I will." He smiled. I turned around and walked downstairs.

"Are you ready now?" my mom asked.

"I think so."

I left the apartment without looking back

Epilogue: One Year Later

I opened the door and went charging after him. He expected it. Once I was in his arms, it felt like old times, not that this had been the first time I had seen him since we departed at Ms. Koneru's apartment. I had seen him three times since then, but they were short visits. Now, it was the summer, and I could spend as much time as I wanted with him.

"You're early," I said. "I wasn't expecting you till tomorrow."

"I couldn't wait that long to see you."

"Aww, you're so sweet!" I said while pinching his cheeks. He hated that.

"Hello, Alex. How about you guys come in now?" my mother tried to seem intimidating even though she liked him. She just didn't want him to know that.

"Yes, Ma'am." He smiled. He walked in with three full suitcases.

"You packed light," I said sarcastically.

"Well, I am staying here for the summer."

"Unfortunately, summer school starts in two weeks for me. If I expect to start strong for my junior year."

"At least you didn't have to go back to school for an entire year like Henry and I."

"True. You'll be alone for a lot of the time though."

"Did you forget everyone is coming in three days for our reunion?" he said sarcastically.

"Shut up! It was a great idea. It will keep us all close. So how is Henry?"

"He's good. He's excited to start MIT next fall. Do you know how Britt feels about it?"

"I honestly don't even know. I still don't understand them. I've never seen two people spend so much time together and claim they're just friends."

"That's how we were at first."

"Yeah, but I liked you the entire time."

Alex laughed. "I can't believe I was so oblivious." He continued to laugh. "Anyway, Henry really just sees her as a sister, and I'm sure she feels the same."

That sounded too familiar. "So is everyone coming to this reunion?"

"Yep! Even Andrew and John."

"Oh. That will be a great time."

"Sure will."

"Do you guys want anything to eat?" my mother asked. She was spying on us.

"No, we're good for right now."

"All right." She closed the door.

"I can't believe I only get the summer with you," I said. I never thought further ahead than now. I knew we had the summer, but I didn't know where everything was going to go from there.

"Actually, you'll be seeing more from me for the next couple of years."

I had no idea what he was talking about. "What are you saying?"

"I'll be attending Auburn next fall." He smiled.

I knew that Alex was going to be apart of my life for a very long time.